The
Good
Doctor

The

John

Simmons

Short

Fiction

Award

University of

Iowa Press

Iowa City

Susan
Onthank
Mates

The

Good

Doctor

The publication of this book is supported by a grant from the National Endowment for the Arts in Washington, D.C., a federal agency.

University of Iowa Press, Iowa City 52242

Copyright © 1994 by Susan Onthank Mates

Library of Congress Cataloging-in-Publication Data

Mates, Susan Onthank, 1950–

The good doctor / Susan Onthank Mates.

p.   cm.—(The John Simmons short fiction award)

ISBN 0-87745-467-1

I. Title.   II. Series.

PS3563.A83538G66   1994

813'.54—dc20   94-18980

                                                                            CIP

98 97 96 95 94 C 5 4 3 2 1

For Joe

Contents

ACKNOWLEDGMENTS

The stories in this collection previously appeared,
in a slightly different form, in the following
magazines: *TriQuarterly* and *Pushcart Prize
XIX*, "Theng"; *Sou'wester*, "Laundry"; *Sunday
Journal Magazine* of the *Providence Journal-
Bulletin*, "Brickyard Pond"; *Collages &
Bricolages*, "My German Problem"; *Innisfree
Magazine*, "Ambulance"; *G. W. Review*,
"These Days"; *Northwest Review*, "East
Providence."
Special thanks to Anita Noble Feng for her insight
and her support.

The
Good
Doctor

Theng

―――――――――

The night Theng Khavang, once a student of litera-
ture, arrived in Providence, the moon split in half and ate itself behind
a passing veil of clouds. His younger brother, Luon, who had lobbied
and bribed unremittingly for five years to get Theng out of Cambodia,
then Thailand, then the Philippines, went to bed, finally, at two in the
morning, because he had to work at six. Luon lay quietly on top of
the blankets, next to his wife Sokunthea, and passed abruptly into
sleep. He dreamt of empty sky, of Theng's gaunt middle-aged face,
of their dead parents, their dead sisters, and of his own life, as irre-
vocably changed as if he had died himself. It was his first dream in
months.

Theng sat on the bare floor of the children's room, smoking a cigarette. The floor was hardwood, the house a solid tenement built for the Irish, but lived in, mostly, by Italians. Savoun, the four-year-old, and six-year-old Chan stared at Theng as he whispered answers to their questions. "I am your father's older brother," he told them. "I lived for five years in Khao I Dang camp. I was born in Battambang, like your father." He talked to the children in matter-of-fact Khmer, but his words flew by them like pelicans lifting off the great lake Tonle Sap.

"What is starving?" asked Savoun. "What is escape? Why aren't you married?"

"Shut up," said nine-year-old Mok. But he listened like the others when Theng ignored him and explained.

And so the names Sisophon, Aranyaprathet, Piopet, and the idea of bachelorhood seeped into the house with the smell of cigarette smoke. Where there had been no photos, no mementos, no heirlooms, no people attached to the words "grandfather," "aunt," "cousin," now there was Theng.

Not that there weren't signals before, omens of memory spelled out in the children's stomach aches at school; in the way Sokunthea, home drunk from the factory in the late afternoons, would curl like a baby on the living room floor; in Luon's sudden pain when, supervising plastic tubing operators and surreptitiously studying for his night class in accounting, he glanced out the dusty windows to see a plane overhead, because he had been about to make fighter pilot, all those years ago. But now there was Theng, come like a premonition into their lives.

At the Refugee Resettlement Office, the worker was unimpressed when Luon pushed Theng forward. "This is my brother," Luon said. "He speaks five languages. He taught university in Cambodia. A good translator."

Outside, Theng said, "No, I can't."

But Luon, the younger son, the one who hadn't been sent to college and had paid ten thousand dollars and promised to keep Theng off welfare said, "You will remember."

They went to Indo-Chinese Social Services, where they knew Luon, because he worked in the Khmer Community Council, and they knew about the problem with his wife; still, there was no job. They went to all the hospitals, the courts, the welfare offices. Once, Luon's old Toyota stopped without warning and they had to walk home through a snow squall, the first Theng had ever seen. That weekend, Luon took Theng to his church and found an overcoat for him in the box of clothes downstairs in the Sunday school. "I've become Christian," he said, and when Theng shrugged his shoulders, Luon added, "you go by yourself now. I can't take any more time from work."

By spring, Theng was translating for the psychiatric social workers who worked outreach for state mental health. He was hired by Refugee Health, but funding was short, so one of them would say, "Hey, Theng, you do French?" and there would be a Haitian family, a woman from Cameroon, French-Canadians from Woonsocket, just north of Providence. The first time Theng tried French, the words stalled and faded in his mouth and even the aide asked if there was something wrong. Theng shook his head. But when he got home, he told the boy, Mok, about the wide and gracious boulevards of Phnom Penh, and the sudden rains that stirred the dust of the sidewalks into clouds.

Most of the time, though, Theng translated for Southeast Asian refugees. Usually, there was a swift and resonant exchange in Khmer, but with the more recent Cambodian immigrants, he spoke slowly, repeating sentences and raising his voice. "Peasants," he told the staff, "look at them, let their kids do anything. Mountain garbage. Khmer Rouge." He pointed out their darker skin, their bare feet, the girls' teased hair. But he made passes at the women, and sometimes when he drove the van from the community center to the clinic, he would arrive a half-hour late, with only one giggling passenger.

The staff ignored it because he was a good translator, even with the Vietnamese and the Hmong, a mountain tribe so stubborn and far from western medicine that they still died of treatable diseases and demon curses, even in Providence. Their language was difficult, and, though Theng pretended to translate, he really spoke to them in signs. The social workers laughed because they could do better themselves.

One day the district supervisor stormed in, shut himself in a room with Theng and shouted so the whole clinic could hear: Don't ever date patients. Don't ever take women in the van by themselves. Don't ever fool around on clinic time. And the outreach workers said to each other, we should have said something, we should have stopped it sooner.

Through all of this, there was the unrelenting work, the stories, four clients an hour, all day. They shot my parents in front of me, my children starved, I was tortured here, and here, look at the scar on my shoulder, my son is blind from a landmine in the forest near the border, oh my husband, he's been that way since he came out of the army, no, I can't have babies, they took out that part, an operation in the Thailand camp, I would have died otherwise. Sometimes Theng would say, this one really has trouble, or, this one just trying for welfare. The clinic staff rushed, complained, joked, drank coffee, and always felt guilty that they didn't stop and weep. But Theng never faltered.

When the police found the apartment empty, one August afternoon after Chan rode his bike into a car and broke an arm, the children said, "Uncle Theng," so they called the clinic. The Department of Children and Families caseworker came that weekend and Sokunthea made tea. Luon pulled a chair out from the kitchen so the woman sat like a queen over them as they squatted on the mat on the floor. They held a cup of sweetened tea up to her and didn't tell her how Sokunthea had been fired for not coming to work, how she was gone for hours from the house and no one knew where, how she began setting an extra place at the table for the baby, when the only baby in the house was the one who died before Luon came back over the border to get her.

"I am president of the Community Council and deacon in the church," said Luon. "My brother is translator for mental health. He used to be a teacher in Cambodia." The caseworker, a fair-skinned young woman, third-generation Irish, told them severely that someone had to be home to take care of the children or they would be taken away. After she left, Luon told Theng he'd seen him on Broad Street hiring a girl, if he wouldn't stop, to get out of his house. Theng laughed and lit a cigarette.

In September Mok was put in the highest track at school, while a note came home concerning Chan, that he was dreaming in first grade. Savoun went to scholarship kindergarten in a private school on the East Side, where she made Play-Doh flowers and beasts in fantastic shapes and colors. After school the children walked a mile from where the bus let them off to the clinic, because Sokunthea was working again, at a jewelry factory out in Pawtucket, three to eleven.

Theng put the children in a back room behind the interview cubicles and told them to do their homework. The clinic knew about his sister-in-law from Community Services, and, besides, the children were always well behaved. Sometimes, when it was raining and no one came, Theng would stand over Mok and touch his books, fingering the paper, slowly reading the text. Once, Mok was reading an English assignment and said suddenly, "Listen, uncle. Isn't it beautiful?" Theng laughed. The boy turned to look at Theng and saw himself reflected in the pool of his uncle's eyes, in the groove of his cheeks, in the sliver of straight black hair that fell across his forehead.

Luon grew busier and busier with the Community Council and the church. He drove the elderly to hospital appointments, he sued a landlord on behalf of Cambodian tenants, and still he worked and went to school. Get on with your lives, he told his people, live for the next generation, try to do good. And, because the past had welled up in him like a tidal wave, he told his own story, over and over. Look what I overcame, he would say, no one had it worse than me, tortured by the Communists, escaped to Thailand, all my friends shot, then arrested by the Thai soldiers, *me*, they thought I was Khmer Rouge, blindfolded, thrown off the truck into the prison yard like a sack of rice, escaped out of prison, back across the border for my wife and baby, how could it be worse? To his wife, he said, you must get over this, pull yourself together. But in the middle of the night, he awoke and watched the moon over the neighbor's roof change from full, to half, to crescent, to fingernail thin, and wept.

In October, Sokunthea drove the Toyota into a side rail on the Newport Bridge and killed herself.

A brittle sheet of ice lay across all of Providence that winter. It was a kind of cold that never seized Cambodia: words froze coming out of Theng's mouth, and Luon, although he'd been in the U.S. longer, stopped moving entirely. Sitting across the kitchen table from each other, the brothers knew, without looking, the way the veins stood out on the other's hands, the way the other's legs crossed narrowly together, the way each other's eyelashes passed, slatted, across their wide-set eyes.

At the clinic, patients slipped and fell coming in the door. The secretary posted a sign, "Watch your step," and so they watched, helplessly, as they fell anyway. The staff had come to Sokunthea's funeral out of respect for Theng. On the way out of the church, one young woman bundled her coat close and said to Theng, her breath clouding her glasses: what can we do, we aren't sure in your culture . . .

And Theng, standing outside in his shirtsleeves unaware of the cold, had turned to her, bewildered. "No," he said, "we are no different."

Luon gave up night classes and church, and stayed home with Chan and Savoun, who would have no one else. He fed them sweetened tea and rice, coconut soup, and spoke to them only in Khmer. "Come on my sweetlings, my little snakes, my fish," he sang to them, until they fell into the bottomless sleep of childhood.

But it was Theng who visited the school on behalf of Mok, in whom grief had taken the form of insatiable studiousness. Look, the boy said, the heart is a muscle that moves blood through the body like a pump. It is divided into four chambers called auricles and ventricles. Archeologists are people who dig for things from the past. They found tablets about ancient kingdoms in the upper Mesopotamia area, which is today northeastern Syria. Maybe a psychiatrist, said the teacher. Maybe if he could talk about his loss. Maybe, said Theng, and left. To Mok, he said, tell me what blood is made of. Tell me where is Syria.

At the clinic, there wasn't time for mourning. A Guatemalan threatened to kill his family, a Liberian woman saw flashing messages in the sky, some swamp Yankees from southeastern Rhode Island brought in their sister who set the house on fire, and through all of this Theng talked and translated and explained Cambodians: the Khmer Rouge came, I starved, my children died, my parents, we escaped across the border, which camp? Khao I Dang, Aranyaprathet, when did they transfer you to the Philippines? How do you pay the rent, go to Indo-Chinese Social Services.

Sometimes Theng left in the middle of an interview and stood outside, smoking a cigarette. By November, he would come to work late smelling of sweat and cheap perfume. When they asked him at work what was wrong, he said "nothing," but once he tried to explain, anyhow: too many words.

He came home late, sometimes not at all. "If you want to go out, why don't you go to night school," said Luon, "instead of whoring." Then the brothers stopped talking to each other.

One night after midnight, Theng rang the doorbell and leaned against the porch, bruised, his clothes ripped, his wallet and keys gone. When Luon answered the door, the two men stood staring at each other until, finally, Theng looked down.

The children rubbed their eyes in the kitchen doorway, watching Luon wash Theng's face and arms. "Go back to bed," said Luon, and they did, unspoken questions gathering like dust in the corners of their room. The next Sunday, Luon started taking the children to church again.

"Our Father," they prayed, "who art in heaven, please give us back our mother."

When Christmas came, Theng went to the Salvation Army and bought a couch and chairs for the living room. He carried them up the stairs himself so it would be a surprise. Savoun jumped on the cushions until Luon stopped her, but even he laughed and thanked his brother. "Theng," he started, and suddenly he remembered Theng's apartment in Phnom Penh with its elegant European furniture and rows of books. Luon had been there only once, because it was a long trip, and he had been a very junior pilot.

"Come," said Theng, "let's take a walk." So they walked down Smith Street together, past the pink and yellow double-deckers, past the 7-Eleven, past the fluorescent glow of the laundromat.

"Do you remember," said Luon, "the smell of our father's pipe?"

"Yes," said Theng.

"And do you remember the new rice, how green it is?"

"Yes," said Theng, looking down at the sidewalk where the ice had melted during the day and refroze when the sun went down.

"Theng," cried Luon suddenly, "why don't I die, too? Why me?"

"I don't know," said Theng. After that, they walked in silence.

The next day, when Theng got home from work, Mok was waiting. "Uncle," he said, as they walked into the apartment. "What is the cerebellum? What makes metal rust? Can I become an archeologist?"

Theng put water on the stove for tea. "You ask too many questions," he said.

"But you're a teacher," said Mok.

"No," said Theng, putting out the cups. "I am not the person who was a teacher. That person is dead."

"My mother is dead," said Mok.

Theng took teabags from the cabinet over the sink and arranged them carefully in the cups. "Yes," he said, then paused for a moment, because he was remembering something he had forgotten. *A la recherche*, he remembered, the silent wingspread of cormorants. Wild ducks flash brilliant orange, green, and red, in and out of the water's edge, snapping at beetles on the surface of the lake. Egrets pick their way through a bristle of water grass, the rattle of cranes in warm evening air. Houses rise up from the water on wooden pilings. A young boy, lying on the floor of a house, drops rice through the cracks and watches the fish swarm up like jewels. The boy grown to a young man, wears leather sandals in the university library. The smell of books.

Du temps perdu, he thought, and the memory of thinking in that way rushed through him. His hand shook as he picked up the kettle, and he recognized the prominent knuckles, the fingers, thin and jointed like stalks of bamboo, the faint crescents rising at the base of the nails. It was the hand of that younger man. "Yes," he repeated. And then he poured the tea.

Laundry

I was folding the baby's diapers—cloth, the kind they make now with a double thickness down the middle—and the phone rang. I was thinking and not thinking; just a second before, the baby had begun to scream that lightning-strike-of-hunger scream, so I was saying to him, wait just a minute let me smooth this crease, and he was shrieking a crescendo and the phone rang. While I was folding and talking to the baby underneath, I was thinking about whether, really, we could afford new bicycles for the girls, the used ones never seem to work quite right, surely it's not such an extravagance, new bikes, but if you've been to Toys 'R Us lately you realize this is a serious issue. On the other hand, I was the fourth child and never had anything new, so I understand that dream, that lust, for something smooth and shiny and unmarked and smelling like paint and not like old garage mildew. So I was thinking: maybe I should try to work another job, after all I am a doctor.

Hi, how are you, yes I'm Dr. Martin, pointing to the name tag that says Dr. Martin on the white coat that says doctor, doctor, doctor. So I hear you're having trouble breathing, pain in your side, a little nausea, the pills bothering you? So sorry to hear about your son, you must take care of yourself, no can tell you for sure that you're going to die, it's a bad disease but there are always exceptions, god, hold my hand god, where in medical school did I miss that course on conviction THIS IS WHAT YOU SHOULD DO MR. DANTIO and me still folding diapers, patting them into squares warm and fresh from the dryer. I don't know Mr. Dantio, the cancer is all over your lungs those cells are eating you, collapsing you, deflating you, your X-ray looks like a drowned man, and each breath drives a spike of pain through your chest. Your wife sits in the corner and hates you and loves you and hates you. I see it in her eyes.

I don't know when can life end, myself I would rather die, but I'm a coward, always have been, I admire your ferocity—I can't help, I can't win this battle, slay the dragon, oh I want to be the hero now, I'll hold your hand Mr. Dantio. I'll watch when you scream and the water in your lungs bubbles up pink like cotton candy from your mouth and nostrils and I'll see the terror in your eyes as you try to pull a breath and your muscles contract and your ribs stand out like a skeleton and no air comes in and your children live three thousand miles away and hate you and love you and your wife is sobbing in the corner. I'm the doctor and I'm supposed to DO SOMETHING, the other doctors say why don't you scope him, biopsy him, give him a hit of chemo, cut him, needle him, anything but don't just let him die and Mr. Dantio I'm not just letting you die, it wasn't my decision, no one asked me should he live or die. But all I can do is watch, I will do that, I will watch even the very end when the air won't come and your fingers claw against the rails on the bed and you said no pain killers doctor, I want to see it coming and I said are you sure oh god.

Do you remember when we first met, and you complained that you itched, and it was flea bites and you had headaches, and it was because your wife yelled at you and you yelled at her, and you would call me in the middle of the night, and I would jump when the phone rang, my husband would groan and roll over in bed, one of the girls would start to cry, and the page operator said with a clothespin clipped on her nose Mr. Salvadore Dantio for you Dr. Martin and I would wake up and you would say, Doctor, that you doctor? Listen, I can't sleep for the itching. And there was nothing wrong with you and I hated you, but in the morning you would say, I'm sorry sorry, things get so bad in the middle of the night and what could I do but laugh, because it's true. The clinic didn't meet every day because I was supposed to do research and teach, I was the first woman doctor at the hospital, I was a role model, I was shiny and new and people whispered, so we met like lovers in the halls and in the lobbies really, you should try to come to your appointments, I said, Mr. Dantio I'll just squeeze you in today meet me on the second floor but next time KEEP YOUR APPOINTMENT and my friends said you'll never get ahead seeing patients in your research time like that, Mr. Dantio there was nothing wrong with you but your wife and your kids and your boss. You put your bony fingers over my hand and said how's a young girl like you a doctor? and I laughed, you drove me crazy. I'm forty Mr. Dantio forty and I don't know how to live and you finally did get something wrong with you Salvadore, you sure did.

The phone is ringing and the baby is crying and I just want to finish folding the diapers so I can balance them on top of the blue and yellow receiving blankets, which is why I didn't use bleach, which I should have because there is a large brown stain on one of the diapers. How did this happen to me? I swore never a housewife, never, never, I won't fall in that black hole, not me.

You grabbed my hand in that cold white room Mr. Dantio and you said I'm a fighter but only if there's a chance all these doctors want to cut me stick tubes in me I don't really understand I'm just a salesman now cake decorations, that's something I understand, you tell me what should I do. And I said I can't tell you that Mr. Dantio, Salvadore, I'm not you. And you said honey I need your help and you made your wife sobbing in the corner leave the room and you looked at me and I thought of you lying in the ICU with tubes in your mouth and arms and lungs and penis and nurses ripping the sheet off and turning your stiff blue body and brushing your hair and calling you sweetie while your blank brown eyes look up at the ceiling, you who never wanted a lady doctor who never wanted to be called sweetie, who always wanted to do the honey-sweetie calling and they're adjusting that tube in your penis and your hairless balls are flopping from side to side and no one even bothers to draw the curtain because your eyes are like mirrors: respirator, manometer, IV pump, electrocardiograph. Your heart keeps going on blip thump, blip thump and your lungs and your liver and your bone marrow filled with infection and your infection is so much like you that we are killing you both together and you asked me what should I do and I couldn't speak. I'm not god. You said well? And you looked out in the hall to make sure your wife wasn't coming in and we were running out of time and I stroked my nine months' pregnant belly and the baby kicked and I said studies show that sometimes if you have this biopsy and we treat you with antibiotics, antifungals, antivirals, you might live longer and you said don't tell me about studies tell me what you would do. And I said studies are important, this is the way doctors know what to do, it's scientific and more systematic than just one doctor's experience, I was good at that stuff even though women aren't supposed to be I knew studies and talked fast clear and incisive and honor society until then I was good at being a doctor. And you said please. I felt my breath clot up somewhere in my throat and I looked at your eyes your ferocious eyes and I said Mr. Dantio, Salvadore I would not do it, don't do it don't let them me do it to you no.

And I couldn't stop the tears, I kissed you and waddled out of the room and stood around the corner so your wife couldn't see me and I cried there right in the middle of the hall with my white coat split down the middle and my belly sticking out, the baby writhing like a snake making ripples in my navy-blue maternity dress with the little red bow on top. The surgeon came up to me, a young man, younger than me, so energetic and clean shaven and he said did you talk him into it? and he ignored the tears and the belly and the baby kicking so unprofessional and I said no.

No! he shouted at me and I said I know as a doctor I should have said do it but as a person I felt no no no and he looked at me and stared at me and finally said there is no difference between how I feel as a doctor and as a person and I saw him with his clean white coat buttoned down his flat front and his neat black hair actually he was a friend of mine I was looking up because he is taller and I said yes I can see that. I should have been angry or distant or something but I wasn't, it would be a lie to say I was—I was feeling no I'm no doctor, I never thickened and rooted and became "Doctor," something's wrong with me, I'm a lost pregnant woman with greasy hair and a discharge in my pants because the baby's coming and I don't know what to do because they never really helped me Plato Aristotle Kant Proust James all I know is this man Salvadore Dantio is dying and I can't do a thing.

I'm still folding the diapers, I have to do a load every day to keep up and the phone is ringing and all I could say Mr. Dantio was that I will be there when your pupils fix and dilate, when your jaw slackens and droops, I'll look though your teeth into the black cavern of your body, I'll smell the diarrhea as your bowels let loose with blood and shit, I'll stay Mr. Dantio, I won't look away. They lied to me about maternity leave and they said well we think you don't really want to be a doctor anyway, you must be conflicted to have a child, want to take two months off, no one sent me flowers they send flowers to all the wives of the doctors but no one sent me anything not even a card when I came back after three weeks still bleeding, I was the only woman doctor in the hospital anyway you never wanted a woman doctor Mr. Dantio, Salvadore, but in the end you looked straight into my eyes, Salvadore and I couldn't lie to you not to you.

I ran into your wife in the supermarket last week over the oranges and she saw me and began to cry and I put my arm around her and tried not to cry myself and she said to me you know when he died that Sunday I tried to call you but they jumped on him and pounded his chest and cut it open and squeezed his heart and he never wanted all of that and she cried and I wondered if she knew that they did it for me, the other doctors, because they knew I didn't want him to die so they couldn't watch him go so they cut him up for me they were embarrassed for me I cared so much I made a spectacle of myself standing in the hall crying. And when they took a piece of his lung, after he died, they found the infection, all I could think of was maybe I was wrong, maybe he could have lived longer if he'd had that biopsy, maybe I never learned this language right, medicine, I feel like I'm a visitor from some other world dressed up like a doctor but they can tell I'm not really one because in moments of great stress I revert to my native tongue. Mrs. Dantio wiped her eyes with the back of her hand and said is that the baby? And she looked at his smooth skin my little son and she smiled and touched the drool on his chin I laughed too.

He's still crying and I pick up the phone and someone says is this the lady of the house? and I don't know what to answer so I think but I still don't know so I hang up and reach for him, he's beginning to make those enunciated baby complaints. I pull up my shirt and my breasts hang out like a cow and just looking at him I feel that sweet pain contraction, the milk spurts and gets us wet. He makes snuffling noises he works his mouth searching for the nipple so I help him wham! he latches on and pulls and the milk is pouring out of both breasts now, I grab a diaper to hold over the other one but it's too late and we're drenched he and I a fecund shower. I know what this means: another load of laundry.

East
Providence

1

The morning her mother was to die, Dora Ramos dreamt she was on the island of Brava, in the year 1492. Although she was not given to historical dreaming, it had been a hard day at the Clip 'N Curl, where she was co-owner, and, as she said later, she wasn't going to fight, for God's sake, a stupid *dream*. She dreamt she was lifting her skirts under the bright Cape Verde stars and wading into the surf, feeling the warm waves lap at her thighs. At the time, she was completely relaxed and content, as she hadn't been for weeks, but she woke to find herself in a puddle of semen.

"Vinnie," she shouted, sitting up and reaching for the Kleenex, "for Christ's sake."

Vinnie Cardoza, her fiancé and partner in the Clip 'N Curl, stirred from his postejaculatory wheezing. "Honeybaby," he said, rolling away from her, "Sugarbuns." He began to snore.

"Oh no you don't," said Dora, leaping from bed and ripping off the blankets. "Look what time it is. Damn it, Vinnie, I ask you, just once, to open for me because I'm late doing the books and—"

"Dorababy," Vinnie blinked apologetically. "You was, you know, moving around."

"I was dreaming," hissed Dora, "about swimming."

"That's nice," said Vinnie, yawning. "You want to go to Florida for vacation this year?"

"Oh God, Vinnie, shut up," said Dora, sitting on the side of the bed and suddenly remembering that her mother was in the hospital.

"Hey," began Vinnie, "don't talk to me that way." But he stopped and put his arm around her when he saw that she was crying.

Dora felt the Toyota spreading out from her like rusted mallard wings. She accelerated down Veteran's Parkway, past the Seekonk River, the rushes and sea grasses of childhood. But when she got to Warren Avenue, any sense of freedom clotted into the shape of customers, idling outside the blank windows of the Clip 'N Curl. Dora pulled up and let Vinnie out, then turned her face resolutely away from the store and toward the weak September sun. Her mother stuck in her thoughts.

"She's okay, I guess," Dora told Vinnie's mother, Tina, later on the phone at the salon reception desk. "They think maybe the cancer spread to her lungs. You know what she said to me on the way there, in the ambulance?"

"No," said Tina. "Tell me." Dora could hear the *thud* and *clunk* of the Seekonk Bowlerama where Tina worked in the background.

"She said," said Dora and stopped, because her tongue suddenly stuck to the roof of her mouth. She was watching Vinnie teasing and talking to the customers, not one of them mad anymore at the shop opening late. How could you not love a man like that? Dora swallowed. "She said," she started again, "she didn't want to miss *Wheel of Fortune.*" Dora began to cry.

"Yeah," said Tina, "Shirley's real big on *Wheel of Fortune.*"

"There she is," said Dora, "hardly able to breathe, and she's complaining about the rescue taking her from her TV."

"You call rescue?" said Tina.

"No," said Dora. "Actually, it was home care the hospital sent out after last time. She blamed me, though. Last thing she said when I left her in the emergency room was Maria wouldn't have brought me here. Made me miss *Wheel of Fortune.*"

"Where is that sister of yours, anyway?"

"Half-sister," said Dora, remembering that Vinnie's mother didn't like any of her family much, them all being Cape Verdean, while Vinnie's mother was from the Azores and considered herself white European. Dora looked down at her hands and thought about America. She could hear Tina saying something but she lost interest and hung up.

"Why'd you do that?" said Vinnie, who'd been waiting for her with a hair-and-skin profile on a client. "You know Momma hates that."

"I was trying," said Dora, "to figure out what you love in her. I mean, why you call that love, you don't really talk to her or anything." She leaned forward, staring at Vinnie.

"Christ, Dora," Vinnie whispered, looking around at the women under hairdryers and reading magazines. Dora didn't take her eyes off him. "Shit," he said finally, "everybody loves their mother."

Dora looked at him, troubled. "Maybe," she said, "we shouldn't get married."

It was then that the phone rang and it was the hospital, to tell her that her mother died.

————————

The funeral was open casket. Shirley looked better in death than Dora remembered her looking in life—cheeks rosy, lips pursed, she lay on her satin cushions as if in bed with a lover. Dora felt unnatural, having such thoughts at her own mother's wake. She felt her nose swell, her eyes begin to fog, and grabbed for Vinnie's arm.

"Take it easy," whispered Vinnie. He patted Dora's hand.

They stood alone next to the casket, because, though Dora put an ad in the paper: *Maria, call home, urgent, your sister Dora,* there had been no response.

"I'm so sorry," said one person after another, leaning close.

"Yes," said Dora.

When they got home, afterwards, Dora sat in the pink armchair near the door and didn't move for a half-hour.

"Dora," said Vinnie, tentatively.

"No," said Dora. She remembered the day they had started dating. He was captain of the wrestling team at East Providence High. She was nothing, except smart. She'd flounced home, wearing his ring like a beacon, but it was too late. Her sister Maria never saw it, she'd left home two years before.

"What do you mean, no?" said Vinnie, sitting on the sofa. "You want something to eat? Want me to get you a soda? A beer? Maybe a slice of pizza?"

"No," shouted Dora. "What I mean is, did you ever sleep with Maria when you were going together?"

"Jesus H Christ," said Vinnie. "That was high school, Dora, high school."

"I'm an orphan now," said Dora.

Vinnie sighed. "Honeybuns," he said, "I love *you.*"

"Love," said Dora. She felt a sudden urge to leave the room but found herself frozen to the chair.

"You think too much," said Vinnie.

Dora climbed the hill to her grandmother's house, which sat stolidly on the hill above Dora's own childhood home. "*Vovo,*" she called, knocking on the peeling green paint. "*Vovo* Regina."

Regina Ramos, a stern mestizo woman of about eighty, rose slowly from her chair and walked heavily to the door. "Dora," she said.

"You did not come to my mother's funeral," said Dora.

Regina waved her hand. She was the mother of Shirley's second husband, Dora's father. She did not like Shirley.

"How do you think I can read your dreams right," she asked, easing herself back into the armchair and pulling a frayed blanket over her thick legs, "when you don't tell me things?"

"It doesn't look like you've cooked for days, *vovo*," said Dora. "I thought those Meals on Wheels people were supposed to come."

"Your mother," said Regina, "made a big mistake when she married into them Lopes family." She reached for a pistachio nut and cracked it with her teeth. "That Maria sister of yours. Big trouble."

Dora looked at her grandmother and felt the hardness inside of herself, its outlines, its stonelike smooth roundness. "Let's not talk about Maria," she said.

"When my son tell me," said Regina, "he going to marry a Lopes widow with a kid, I tell him you better not. Them Lopes all come from a brother-sister marriage, way back, you know what I mean? Kicked out of Portugal, come to Cape Verde, then kicked out of Cape Verde."

"*Vovo*," said Dora, sighing.

"You know she have the devil sign on her feet. That's why she caused my son, your father, so much trouble."

"I know she has a little skin between her toes." She suffered a sudden stab near her heart at the image of Maria, dancing barefoot in their room, laughing. She must have been about twelve; Dora, nine.

"He had it too, Manuel, the father. Them Lopes, all of them oversexed on account of it."

"Have you eaten today?" said Dora.

Regina watched Dora from the sides of her eyes. "Something's going to happen. I been dreaming steady now, since Shirley died. Old dreams. You been dreaming them too."

Dora shook her head. "I haven't dreamed nothing," she said. She walked out to the kitchen and began doing the dishes.

"Shirley willed everything, the house and all, to you," called Regina from the living room. "She told me she done it, not nothing to Maria." She cleared her throat. "You better think, Dora. What you going to do about that?"

"What you need to do," said Vinnie, stroking her hair, "is find Maria." He looked at her earnestly. "You don't got no problem loving. Trouble is, you loved your sister, and your mom kicked her out."

Dora turned and looked at him. "Vinnie," she said. "Why do you put up with me?"

"Come on Dora," said Vinnie. "You're just a little knocked outa whack by your Mom dying and all." When Dora didn't answer, he added, "You know, when *Vovo* Regina starts on her dream shit about them bastards and devil marks and all, I figure, you know, she's a nut case. But *you* start thinking about—now let me see, that could be this Spanish Inquisition stuff, that could be Columbus. You gotta kiss it off more. Relax."

"Vinnie," said Dora, "I love you."

"I figure," said Vinnie, blushing, "that if we hit every bar, every club and McDonald's here and in Providence, maybe Seekonk, too, Maria'll turn up. We'll just look until we find her."

"I'm afraid she's living on the streets," said Dora, "turning tricks."

"Maybe she is," said Vinnie. "So what?"

"Yes," said Dora, beginning to cry. "So what."

2

"So," said Maria Lopes, sometime supermarket checker, sometime whore, speaking to her half-sister, Dora, "—you come to tell me the old lady croaked?" She flicked her cigarette ashes on the sidewalk. "Big fucking deal."

"She was your mother, too," said Dora.

Maria didn't answer. She leaned back against the building. "I hear," she said, "you and Vinnie gettin' married."

"Yes," said Dora.

"That weenie," said Maria, laughing.

"Listen," said Dora, looking away from her sister's face and down at her leather skirt and laddered black stockings. "I'm sorry, Maria, for whatever happened."

"Ooh," said Maria, stubbing out the cigarette with her patent-leather spike heel, "that is *so* reassuring." She looked at Dora. "You always was a pompous little dorkhead."

"You know," said Dora, "I used to look in the mirror and try to copy the way you smiled."

"Isn't that a fucking bitch?" said Maria. "Their precious kid wanting to be just like me?"

"You want," said Dora, after a minute, "to come live with me, Maria? Please?"

Maria leaned her head against the brick wall. Then she began to tap her forehead with her fist. "You, me, and Vinnie, in his apartment. I didn't think you was so liberated." She laughed.

"Well, I was thinking," said Dora, pulling her jacket closer around her, "about Mom's house. She willed it, you know, to me."

"So I hear," said Maria.

"But," said Dora, "I want to give it to you."

Maria stared at her for a minute. "I get it," she said. "Your grandma *vovo* shithead tried that a long time ago."

"Tried what?" said Dora, stamping her feet to keep warm.

"Get me to shut up about what your Dad done to me."

"I'm giving you the house because it was *your* father that bought it," said Dora.

"We was talking," said Maria, "about *your* father."

"You come to the lawyer's office at two next Wednesday, and I'll deed it over," said Dora. "You going to be there?"

"He raped me," shouted Maria. "When I was ten."

Dora stared at her. "You're making it up," she said.

"Yeah," said Maria. "I tried to tell your *vovo* Regina 'bout it, too. What a big fucking mistake."

"Stop it, Maria," said Dora, starting to shake. "You always did like to say horrible things just to hurt people."

"So don't believe it," said Maria, shrugging her shoulders. "See if I care. Just don't ask me to be sorry when any of them croak." She opened her purse and pulled out a pint of whisky. "I," she said, wiping the lip of the bottle with her thumb, "used to think my real daddy was going to save me. Call up the water, like your precious *vovo* was always saying he could. I spent my life looking out that window in that fucking house, waiting on him."

"Maria," said Dora, "don't drink that."

"Go away," said Maria. She waved at a passing pickup truck.

"You going to take the house? Please?" said Dora.

"I don't need no house," said Maria. "I got fish toes, remember? I'm waiting for my fish-daddy." She took a long drink from the flask, then wiped her lips with the back of her hand. "Manuel," she called in falsetto, "come get your baby-girl."

"Don't you remember," said Dora, "how we used to hide from Mama in our room, and we used to dance from the radio?"

"My congratulations to Vinnie," said Maria, "Vinnie the weenie. And to his Momma Tina. She still got a ramrod up her ass?"

"This Wednesday," said Dora. "At two."

3

Three weeks later, Maria awoke, late, and without make-up, to an extraordinary tide and the smell of rotting bluefish rising up the See-konk River. As she slid from the bed and crossed to the window, a hot wind slipped through the old tenement house to eddy around her feet, whispering by the slight but tough webbing of skin between her first and second toes.

"Lopes blood runs true," said Tina, Vinnie's mother, to the rest of the bowling alley ladies, as if in revelation. But everyone already knew that the reason Maria's mother Shirley had thrown her out at fourteen was this mortal resemblance to her father, the late Captain Manuel Lopes. And the fact that she'd been found, her white body glinting over the ten-feet marker, swimming naked with the coach in the East Providence YMCA.

The house in which Maria had spent the night was a dingy-brown triple-decker from the twenties, built by Cape Verdeans when you could walk the covered bridge from the river's east bank back to India Point, before the highway split the community the way the water never had. This house had been bought for Shirley Lopes Ramos by her first husband so she could look longingly out the window over the railroad tracks, the marshy shore, and across the tidal Seekonk river to the pier off India Point where, four times a year, Manuel docked his packet ship, the *Belmira*. On her death, Shirley willed the house and her estate in its entirety to her daughter by her second husband, Dora Ramos, and made no mention of Manuel or her eldest daughter except to say, in the words of Jay Goldstein, her downtown lawyer, that this omission was intentional and did not come about through oversight.

So it was, everyone later agreed, her own disinherited childhood bed in the triple-decker house from which Maria arose that morning and went to the window to watch the brown waves tossing tires, plastic soda bottles, driftwood, dead fish, tampon applicators, and pale coils of used condoms over the cracked retaining wall and onto the roses and grapevines of her dead mother's backyard. And, beyond a doubt, behind her, as she climbed out the window and walked down to the river to drown herself, lay a white lump: her half-sister Dora's fiancé, Vinnie Cardoza, tangled in the sheets.

Rushing to work at the Clip 'N Curl from where she parked her car on School Street, Dora stumbled over the armored shells of horseshoe crabs, scattered across the sidewalk. She rubbed her eyes, took out the key to the shop, and was trying to fit it in the lock, when she saw, suddenly and clearly reflected in the window, that there were too many people in East Providence. Italian, Cape Verdean, Azorean, Dominican, they were loitering on the corners, dressed for work, her neighbors drinking paper cups of coffee from the Donut King down the street.

Dora paused for a minute, thinking of her haste to give their childhood house back to Maria. She did it to absolve herself of their mother's favoritism. No, she told herself, she did it to disassociate herself from her sister, who it had taken Dora three days to find after Shirley's death, and who she suspected of whoring, using, and general low-class behavior. She supposed that the problem lay with Maria's pale Portuguese skin and bony nose, so evocative of seafaring, in a family that was solid Crioulo. Then she sighed, because it didn't make any difference now, with all of them, both fathers and the mother dead. A cold damp broke into her thoughts, and, looking down, she saw she stood in an inch or two of water, the stiletto heel of her purple ankle-boot stabbed cleanly into a clump of yellow seaweed.

Later, when she could talk about it, she said that, even then, she knew the flooding of the I-195 bridge into Providence had some meaning, but at the time all she could think of was their orphanhood, hers and Maria's, and that feeling made her pound harder on the door to the salon. "Vinnie," she called, "open up. Vinnie honey," because she thought her fiancé had spent the night helping his mother hang wallpaper, and should've been there, already, checking the combs and brushes, stacking the magazines, and getting ready to open.

"Don't tell me it was any of Vinnie's fault because you're wrong," said Tina Cardoza, patting her sprayed grey hair and sliding onto the bench at the head of lane 3 in the Seekonk Bowlerama. She was second generation from the Azores, and conscious of her condescension to talk in such familiar terms to Dora's grandmother Regina Ramos, who was—as she preferred to think of Cape Verdeans—African, even though the Ramos family owned a bakery, a fish market, and this very bowling alley. "That Maria was a whore, I seen her myself down in New Bedford walking the streets." She lit up a cigarette and picked at her nail. "Maybe I protected him too much, raising him up you know what I mean?"

Regina sat in her wheelchair, where the senior-citizen van had left her that morning, and looked at Tina dispassionately. "I think," she said, "maybe Dora calls the wedding off."

"Well maybe," said Tina, raising her voice, "Vinnie's going to call it off, and not a bad idea anyway, seeing as how he's got a better look at what he's marrying into."

They sat for a moment with the balls rolling and clunking around them. Then Regina said, "Good look all right, better look than God entitles him to, his own about-to-be sister-in-law. Didn't he never see her feet? You don't do *that* to no Lopes girl."

"She was a slut," said Tina, smashing out her cigarette. "Good riddance."

But Regina turned first, looking out over the lanes. "What do you know?" she said. "Almost got the whole city drowned, your boy did." She crossed herself, then closed her eyes and went to sleep.

And there, snoring faintly in the Seekonk Bowlerama, Regina Gomes Ramos dreamt of her own childhood, of her grandmother's rolling voice as she told Regina about the Portuguese gentleman who arrived with his wife on the last leeward island of Brava, before there were fields or markets or even African slaves. See, says Regina's grandmother, gesturing as she carefully cranks water from the village well, see with what arrogance he stained his boots with Brava dust, how he scowled at this rock in the sea. And Regina sees him building the house on the cliff for his snotty lady and sees the black-haired children, those first feral creatures of the land, little weasel-nosed brats. And when Regina awakes, she feels old, and still dreaming. She touches her cheeks, her arms, her legs and feels dust, dust and decay.

And she thinks of the girl she betrayed, the girl her son was step-father to and forced into his bed, the girl who drowned herself. She thinks of Maria.

"She told me one time," said Dora, lying in bed and stroking Vinnie's thigh, "how her real father walked to her, you know, across the water."

"Oh Baby," said Vinnie, moving her hand higher, "don't stop."

Dora pulled her hand away and rolled over to stare up at the stars painted on the ceiling. After she moved in with Vinnie, she took one whole day off from work to pry down Vinnie's mirrored tile, then painted it over in midnight blue with constellations, Little Dipper, Big Dipper, Orion, Andromeda. She got them out of a book from the public library, but she remembered most of them anyway, from when her father took her with him to open the bakery and start up the bread, four in the morning, and the windows all fogged over.

The stars are different here, he would tell her, not like Cape Verde. And then he fell silent. That was what she remembered the most about him, his sadness, and the way, after Maria ran away, he would leave the bakery in mid-morning, get in the car with a loaf of bread and a covered Tupperware bowl of chicken-rice soup, then return empty handed. I should die, he told Dora, when they were alone. I am not a good man. When Dora was ten, and Maria thirteen, he did die, crashing into the pastries with a fist clutched to his chest.

"She was looking out that window, the one in her room," said Dora dreamily, "when she saw him, her real father, coming across the river, waving and picking his nose."

"Dora," said Vinnie, "Baby," rolling on top of her and sucking on her ear.

"Stop it Vinnie, this is serious," said Dora.

"Oh shit," sighed Vinnie and rolled off. "Who cares what happened to Maria when she was ten years old."

"Vinnie," shouted Dora, sitting up. "Don't you think I saw you standing there in my house, just watching her go into the river? Half-naked, don't you think everyone knew what you'd been doing?" She began to cry.

Vinnie stared at her. "Hey," he said, clearing his throat. "You gave that house back to her." He shook his head. "Besides, I thought we was finished with all that."

Dora pulled her knees up to her chest. "I should've dove in after her," she whispered. "It's all my fault." She began to cry and Vinnie tried to put his arm around her, but she shook him off.

"She didn't mean nothing to me, it was the wine," said Vinnie. "Honest. I don't know why she went running out. If I'd known that, I'd have dove in myself."

"My own sister," said Dora. "Oh God."

"She hated you," said Vinnie. Dora stopped sniffing and stared at him. "Why'd you *think* she did it?" he said.

The governor declared East Providence a disaster area and applied for federal funds. There was several million dollars' worth of damage to waterfront properties, but worst hit were the underpinnings of the I-195 bridge, which had cracked in subtle but irremediable ways. The traffic tie-ups lasted for months. Only after events slowly faded back into normality did less dramatic incidents appear in the *Providence News*. "Witnesses reported," read a small item on the East Bay page a few months later, "that at the height of the storm surge, a young woman climbed out her window, walked down the hill, across the railroad tracks, and into the Seekonk River. The woman, who drowned, has been identified as Maria Lopes of East Providence. A large number of onlookers were present."

They're painting us all like criminals, said several of the neighbors. But now, with such a blunt and public statement in the press, rumors hardened, and each tried to understand his own position in the shape and meaning of things. "I think," said Maura Centazzo, the Bowlerama cashier, to Alba Ramos, Dora's cousin, "she was trying to walk back to her real Daddy, and you know how he hated that I-195 bridge, ruined his business." Over dinner at the Mandarin Gardens, two blocks from Shirley Lopes Ramos's ravaged house, the high-school principal said to his wife, "Between you and me, she did it for spite, just stirring the pot. Same way she seduced that boy Hector, remember him? Coached the scholarship team down at the Y? Dropped out of college on account of the whole thing, poor kid." And the East Providence YMCA announced water-safety classes, including lifesaving. "Never again," said the Y's director, "will anyone not know what to do in such a tragic situation."

Although he wasn't asked, Jay Goldstein gave a formal statement to the police about Maria's actions two weeks before her death. According to Mr. Goldstein, at the deeding, which occurred in his office, Dora, the half-sister, seemed quite nervous, but Maria was smiling a small dreamy smile. "Sure," she said, almost tenderly, when Mr. Goldstein explained the transfer, "Fucking bitch, ain't it, how things turn out?" And when they left, she turned to Dora and said, "Congratulations again on you gettin' married." When Dora didn't reply, she added, as if in explanation, "You really should've kept the house."

"I got a call," said Tina, Vinnie's mother, who was at the Bowlerama and couldn't stop talking once she got started, "my friend Connie works down at the Tavares Bar and Grill, she told me to get my boy outta there before he got into trouble, he was drinking with Dora's sister." Actually, Connie said later to the other waitresses, the boy was drunk and hanging all over the girl, but she wasn't drinking at all, just looking kind of thoughtful.

None of this reached Regina Ramos, who, in her eighty-fourth year, having survived her husband, her son, her daughter-in-law, and now her step-granddaughter, became increasingly short of breath. She was lying under a blanket on the couch, the television on without sound. "It had to stop," Regina said to herself, feeling the tightening in her chest, the age reaching in to strangle her. "He was a good boy." No, it was her husband she was telling, about their boy, and his stepdaughter, what she had never told him, what she saw, how she called Child Welfare that day, on her own son. "They came, wanted to take her out of the house, it wasn't his fault, she looked like a woman, already at ten." She waved fiercely at the corner of the living room, to see who was standing there, those gossipy women, came to market and talked all day, how she hated them, how she hated the claustrophobia of the islands. Another sharp pain clenched her chest, and she remembered herself at ten, "Oh my God," she said, and she realized that she wasn't home anymore, but here, dying in her living room in East Providence. "Child," she whispered, "forgive me."

"As God is my witness, she wanted it as much as I did," said Vinnie to the assistant manager of the Clip 'N Curl, as they were cleaning up in the back. "Besides, we spent the whole night talking about her family in Cape Verde." He dumped a basket of hairbrushes into a cerulean blue disinfectant. "She stared so long out that window, I almost went back to sleep, it took me a while to react, you know what I mean, when she just slid it open and climbed out, stark naked. Like I was still asleep, I went after her, and there was the water coming up to the house, and people standing in it, dressed up, talking, in the other yards, and out in the street, just like they was waiting for something. And she's walking slow, down to the tracks, but not wading like the rest of us, but walking *on* it, like you can see her white feet on the brown water, and the rest of her gorgeous, smiling, walking, and all of us stuck." He turned to look at the assistant manager. "Shit," he said, "I think about it every day, the way we couldn't move, like we been *called* there to watch. And everyone was there, Dora, and my mother, everyone from the bowling alley. She wasn't no angel," he said suddenly, "she was getting off on it, smiling at Dora, turning, smiling at me. But the weirdest thing was the water, the way it came twisting up around her legs and sliding down her tits, like she was calling it, like it was her lover, *intimate*, like we shouldn't be watching." Vinnie went over and started stacking hair dryers. "Anyway," he said, "by the time we figured out what was happening, it was too late. She just went under."

The next morning, Alba, Dora's cousin from the Bowlerama, called Vinnie's apartment to speak to Dora, because no one knew she wasn't living there any more. "Dora," Vinnie said softly, as he slid through the door of the water-damaged house in which she had grown up. She was standing barefoot in the living room. "*Vovo* Regina's real sick. They think she's gonna die maybe." But Dora looked up at him as if he were a complete stranger. "Please, Dora," said Vinnie, "come back. Don't be staying here all alone. I miss you."

"*Vovo*," thought Dora, and she was seized by Regina's ongoing dream: it is 1492, the parish priest hikes slowly up to the house on the cliff and says to the gentleman, you must allow me to baptize the children, and there is an argument, but finally the priest is standing in the small church holding the first, the wailing infant. The priest cries out, almost dropping the baby, and he looks down at the other children's feet. Yes. Webbed. All of them. That very day comes the answer to his letter to Lisbon: brother and sister, the gentleman and his wife.

"I can't come back, Vinnie," said Dora, coldly interrupting the dream, even though she knew Regina was dying and running out of time. "I don't believe in nothing anymore. Not us, not the Clip 'N Curl, not nothing." Vinnie tried to answer, but he saw that Dora was looking away from him, out the window.

The villagers call for auto-da-fé, but the priest looks at his congregation, Sephardim, Iberian rebels, Portuguese businessmen, Fula, Mande, and Balante slaves, mulatto children of all shades, and he knows that one of them will sail on the third voyage of Cristobal Colon, and it won't be off the edge of the world, or perhaps it will be the edge of the world as they have known it, and the edge will be called America. And, so the priest says, Cast them from land, from a place among people, but give them the sea. Who are we to judge what hand marks the innocent feet of a child?

"Shut up, vovo," shouts Dora, affronted more than she can bear by Regina even dreaming the word "innocent."

But Dora sees the priest's vestmented arm among the many pushing off the small boat, feels the water lapping up against her ankles. "Why don't you just die and get it over with," she says to Regina. Then she begins to weep. "Maria," she cries, "Maria. It was all my fault." But, looking around her mother's house, she sees guilt seeping everywhere, right down to the foundation.

After Vinnie leaves, she goes to the basement and gets a can of paint. Then she covers the damaged ceilings, the walls, even the water-rotted floors with stars. She is alone now, with her hate and her love, so she is carefully scientific. The house is in East Providence, but the constellations are those of a winter night in Cape Verde. They are beautiful, she thinks, innocent and filled with sorrow. They are clear enough to navigate by.

The
Good
Doctor

Some years ago, during a winter that drove even the thieves and addicts indoors, Helen van Horne arrived to run the medicine department at City Hospital. Born in Wisconsin and just returned from Africa, she expected to feel at home in the South Bronx.

"Why," she asked Diana, as they rounded on the men's ward after a meeting of the community board, "do they hate me, so soon?"

"You look very clean," said Diana kindly, "your blouses are always white." She didn't add, you are so pale, your blue eyes so light they seem a disfigurement. Diana Figueroa was the medical chief resident for the year.

"Are you married?" asked Helen, noticing the gold band on Diana's smooth brown finger. "Yes," said Diana, and Helen imagined a home, two children, and a swing set. When Helen chose medical school, the act implied spinsterhood. Aware of her attractiveness, she tried but found herself unable to offer the standard plea for forgiveness: my patients, my students will be my children. Instead, she swept behind the parents who disapproved, the wedded college classmates, the condescending but lecherous professors, in the dust of her flight to Africa.

"What does your husband do?" she asked Diana.

"He said he wanted to be a lawyer." Diana finished writing in a chart, signed her name, and handed it to Helen.

"Oh," said Helen. "I suppose one of you might have to work part-time." She tried to imagine herself, when she was a young doctor, coming home at eight or nine in the evening, on her day off call, to talk to a child instead of throwing herself into bed.

"One of us does work part-time," said Diana. "When he works at all." She laughed. "Men," she said.

Helen began reading the chart. "I suppose that's fine, then," she said. She countersigned Diana's note, which was incisive and succinct. I will help this chief resident, she thought. She is smart, like I was, and young enough to be my daughter. It pleased Helen to think of a daughter, married and a doctor.

In Tanzania, Helen ran a dispensary, single-handed, far into the bush. She operated by automobile headlight, diagnosed by her senses alone, tended the roses next to her well, and learned the language of solitude. "A good summer," she wrote to her sisters. "Not too much malaria, I've got the women to allow tetanus vaccination, now if only the generator doesn't break down again." She had two brief love affairs, otherwise the years passed from grassy summer to muddy winter to grassy summer like figures of a dance.

She slipped into relationship with the Masai and the earth: she cleaned the clinic each sunrise, ordered seasonal supplies with the solstice, and stopped numbering days entirely. She menstruated on the full moon, and the villagers came when they came, appearing unexpectedly on the horizon, carrying their sick in hammocks slung horizontally between tall men. After fifteen years, Helen described Tanzanian mountain fever in a clear and intelligent communication to the British journal *Lancet*, and because the virus was isolated from her specimens, and because it was interesting in its mode of replication and transmission, Helen's name became known.

On the day she received the letter from City Hospital, Helen folded it carefully into her skirt pocket, slung the rusted clinic shotgun on her back, and took the long path over the ridge. When she had first set up, the missionary nuns who preceded her said to always take the jeep. Lions, they warned earnestly, shaking their heads. Elephants. Rhinoceros.

Helen sat on a rock and watched a pair of gazelles leaping across the bleached grass on the other side of the ridge. In the distance, a giraffe swayed against the trees. I live in a garden of Eden, she thought, why would I ever want to leave? She looked down the way she had come, to the tin roof of her clinic. It was such an insignificant mark on the land, so easily removed. She traced the varicosities on her leg and felt suddenly afraid.

And so Diana became the guide of her return, pointing out the snow that bent the branches of the blue spruce whose roots cracked through the concrete of the long-abandoned formal entry to City Hospital. "I grew up on Willis Avenue," Diana told her, as they sat in the cafeteria.

"I grew up on a farm near Madison," Helen replied, "but my parents are dead. There's no one who knows me there now."

They sat for a moment, surveying the crowd of people, the yellowed linoleum, and the sturdy wooden tables. "Three types of students rotate here: do-gooders, voyeurs, and dropouts sent by the Dean," said Diana. She nodded down the table and Helen saw an extraordinarily beautiful young man with smooth, almost hairless golden skin, laughing and tossing his head. Like the African sun, thought Helen. Like sex.

"Mike Smith," said Diana. "A real goof-off. Kicked out everywhere else, the patients complained." Helen looked down at her lunch, conscious of her grey hair and how long it had been since she worked with men. She stared at the boiled tongue and sauerkraut.

"You'll get used to it," said Diana, "some of the cooks are Puerto Rican, some are from the South."

Helen took a bite of the meat. "I'll write a letter to the Dean," she said, "about that boy. These patients deserve consideration, too. A failing student should be failed."

"It won't," said Diana, "do any good."

Helen studied Diana's smooth face, her soft black eyebrows, and her neatly organized list of patients clipped to the board next to her lunch. "I hope you have enough time with your husband," said Helen. "I hope you decide to have children, soon, before you get too old."

In the afternoon of the day she came, Helen carried her two suitcases up to the staff quarters and sat on the narrow bed. There was a single bureau in the room, battered but solid oak, standing at a slight tilt on the warped linoleum. In the top drawer she found a tourniquet, a pen, index cards, and several unused needles. She picked them out carefully and dropped them into the garbage, then lined the drawer with paper towels from the sink. Folding her skirts into the bottom drawer, she found a package of condoms, tucked into the back right corner.

The window stuck several times before it finally creaked all the way up. Car horns, salsa music from the local bar, sirens, the sooty yearnings of urban life blasted into the room. Helen wrapped her arms around herself and stood, considering. She looked across at the decaying curve of the expressway, traffic crowded like wildebeest during mating season in the Serengeti. Then, turning back to the task of unpacking, she noticed faint fingernail scratches, hieroglyphics of passion, etched on the green wall at the head of the bed.

Over the next few months, Dr. Helen van Horne took charge of the department. She reviewed charts, observed procedures, met everyone including housekeepers and orderlies. "What disinfectant do you use?" she asked. "Why is this man waiting so long at X-ray?" She was on the wards at five in the morning and eleven at night, her faded hair pulled into a ponytail, starting an intravenous at a cardiac arrest, checking the diabetics' drawers for candy. Sometimes, standing in front of a washbasin, or sitting at a deserted nursing station at the change of shift, she would suddenly find herself watching the papery skin on the backs of her hands. What do I have to show for the years? she asked herself, but then a young woman gasping from rheumatic heart disease, or an old man bent with cancerous metastases passed by her, and she told herself: it doesn't matter. And she got back to work.

"What are they doing?" she asked Diana, as they passed a window looking toward the inner courtyard of the hospital. Michael Smith, the contours of his back glistening in the heat, kicked a ball toward some other students, boys and girls, who were encouraging several small children to kick it back.

"Oh," laughed Diana, "he's too much, isn't he?"

"The children will pull out their IVs," said Helen.

Diana walked around to the door. "Mr. Smith," she called, "the children will pull out their IVs."

"*Anything* you say Dr. Figueroa," said the boy.

"He played football for Harvard," said Diana, apologetically, when she came back inside.

"When you are a teacher," said Helen, looking back to check on the children but involuntarily glancing at Michael Smith's tight buttocks, "you must be careful about personal relationships. There is the issue of abuse of power." She looked away quickly, and with humiliation.

"Yes," said Diana. "But," she added, "the men do it all the time."

After that, Helen gave the teaching of the students over to Diana. She herself spent even more hours attending research meetings at the medical school and supervising the medical service. She set up studies and chaired meetings. She read textbooks of molecular biology. "We are beginning to see a new syndrome of infections in IV drug users," she said in conference, and felt her power as the other doctors listened, because she was the Helen van Horne of Tanzanian mountain fever. She was senior and spoke with authority of microbial isolation and immune alterations. She submitted scholarly articles, and her roots spread into this identity, Chairman of Medicine at City Hospital. She stood taller, her walk grew firmer.

Once, she brought Diana with her to the medical school, to listen to her lecture. Afterwards, the men in the audience, who were division chiefs, but not department chairmen, spoke to her carefully and politely. The dean, who was the same age as Helen, came up to tease her about her theories, and Helen, who had, despite herself, imagined the touch of his hands and the feel of his skin, caught each barb and sent it back, leaning against the podium and laughing. But when she introduced Diana to him, he widened his stance. When Diana said how much she admired his research, he put his arm around her and introduced her to the other men, who, one after another, smiled with authority and watched her smooth brown cheeks.

Helen threw herself into work. "Examine these patients and report to me," she told the students. "Tell me if they are rude," she told the patients, "tell me if you think they will make good doctors," and the women always remarked on Michael Smith. Oh, they said, his hair, his eyes, his body. "He's careless," snapped Helen to Diana, "missed diagnoses, wrong medications." But when the boy stood to be rebuked, Helen felt the speculation in his eyes. She tightened her lips. "If you don't work, I will fail you, don't think I won't," she told him. But he glanced at her breasts and her nipples hardened.

"I don't want to be any superdoctor," he said, looking at her seriously. "I want to enjoy my life, you know what I mean?"

She laughed, because she had felt that way, too, then walked away. You are a fifty-year-old woman, she told herself. You are inappropriate. You are disgusting.

Later, on the wards, she rounded with Diana and set stern rules. "No more than six units of blood *per* bleeder," Helen said, after she watched an intern run ten units into a cirrhotic.

"But he's a young man," said Diana.

"He'll vomit up twice as much tomorrow," said Helen. "We don't have enough blood." She felt a pleasure in teaching this resident, after all the years of solitude. The girl would be a good doctor, she thought, but she needed disappointment.

"City Hospital," read the dean's reply, "has always been an albatross to the Medical School." It was spring now, and Helen watched the cornflowers pushing up through the cobbled ramp leading to the ambulance bay. She wondered if the dean had ever seen an albatross. Wingspan as wide as a man's arms, Daedalus, Icarus, she thought, and remembered the bird that followed them all the way from Dar es Salaam to Madagascar. Her lover was Indian, son of the supply ship's owner, a merchant in Dar. "Look," he said to her, as they were making love. His gold neckchain lay fallen in a spray of sweat from his dark chest onto hers, looped around one pink nipple. "You belong to me," he said. That was when her skin was smooth and firm, her hair a pale sheet of gold. She had wished, suddenly, and just for a moment, that a child, his child, would seed and grow in her womb. A year later, he was gone.

Helen fell into the rhythms of the Bronx. She met with Diana each morning and each evening. "The students," said Diana, "are improving."

"They need to be taught to do good," said Helen. "You are teaching them by example." She surprised herself. She had avoided a moral vocabulary. These had been the words of distance between herself and her parents: duty, family, obligation.

But Diana smiled and slicked back her hair. She had begun to wear it in a ponytail, too, a thick curly fall to complement Helen's thin fair one.

"Stick in the mud," Michael Smith teased her. "Dr. van Horne, Jr." He'd become friendly with the head of housekeeping, a middle-aged black man from Yonkers, and the two of them sat on the steps outside the emergency room talking football and joking, catcalling women as they walked by.

Diana stopped in front of him. "You left a patient in the hall last night and went off without signing him out. When I *just happened* to come by, he was already going into diabetic coma."

Michael Smith paled. "I'm sorry," he said.

"Tell it to the patient," said Diana, and left.

"But is he okay?" called Smith. She didn't answer.

Everyone in the hospital knew and respected Helen now. "Good morning, Doctor," she was greeted by the man who ladled out the scrambled eggs. "Good evening," by the woman mopping the women's ward. Sometimes the Spanish workers slipped and called her "Sister" when they stopped to thank her for taking care of a relative. Helen would glance at her own upright reflection in the glassed doors, curious to see how she might be mistaken for a nun.

She became convinced that this was how the people of the hospital saw her, as a nun, a medical missionary to the South Bronx. Bride of Christ, she taunted herself, standing in her room one night as the moonlight spread across the floor and crept up her ankles. Spinster

Mother of City Hospital. How had this happened to her? That night she plaited her sheets into dreams: her nails became claws; her arms, wings of a nun's habit; and she felt the spring air rustle her belly as she swooped on a creature, garbage rat, skittering city mouse, swallowing its body with one snap while its head lay severed and bleeding on the ground.

Yes, she told herself, waking the next morning. The meaning of her years in Africa came to her suddenly as if in revelation. Apprenticeship. Learning to subjugate her will. She would dedicate herself to the patients and the students of City Hospital. Her face took on a pregnant glow, and she felt more content than she could remember in her life.

Because the dean would not remove Michael Smith, Helen decided she would make him into a doctor. She gave most of the teaching duties to Diana, but she no longer avoided the boy. To Diana she said, "You must think of how you will fit your practice around your family, and how you will choose a job where your husband can find work too." Diana smiled but said nothing. To Michael Smith, whom she caught leaving the hospital at five, with a blood sugar left unchecked, she said, "You must do whatever is necessary for the patients' good, even if it means you don't eat, don't sleep, or don't leave the hospital."

Smith flushed slightly, then looked over her left shoulder at a flurry of young nurses who were leaving, too, and said, "I'm going into radiology."

"Good," said Helen. "You'll make money. But first, you must pass your medicine rotation." As she walked away, she felt his eyes on the sway of her hips. Students, she told herself, become infatuated with the power of their teachers. Later that night, sitting at the bedside of a dying man, a drug addict infected on a hole he had eroded in his heart, Helen felt herself strengthen and harden in conviction. None of the private hospitals taught the concept of service. It was here the boy would learn to be a doctor, and it was her responsibility to teach him.

The third week of May began the wave of deaths. Death was of course a familiar presence at City Hospital, but like a wild tide, people began dying in unprecedented numbers. First, it was several cardiac failures on the men's wards, then a medication allergy on the women's ward, then one of the drug rehabilitation doctors fell out of a closet one morning, curled in the fetal position with a needle in his arm and stone-cold dead.

Helen called a meeting of the hospital's physicians. "I can't find a pattern," she said, "but I feel a connection, somewhere underneath." She didn't add, and I feel somehow responsible.

The next day *Staphylococcus* broke out in the neonatal nursery, crops of pustules erupted on even the heartiest of infants. Helen stood outside the plate glass of the babies' ward and watched the nurses wrap a tiny corpse, folding the blanket around the child, a flannel shroud. Why, she asked herself, because even Africa had not prepared her for the speed and the sweep of these deaths. Overcome, she paced the streets outside the hospital, walking blindly past the rubble, the garbage, and the deserted streets, in the long twilights of the late spring.

But the final straw was Henry, the chief of maintenance who sat, sighed, and fell over one day at dinner. It was Michael Smith who leapt on his chest and screamed, "Help," because he'd been sitting with Henry, once again, playing poker when he should have been drawing the evening bloods on the men's ward. They all came, residents, students, Helen, Diana. They ran a code in the cafeteria just as they would have in the emergency room: hooked up the EKG machine, pumped the chest, breathed in the slack mouth, started several large-bore IVs, and called to each other pulse, medication, paddles, step back, shock. But it was different, thought Helen, as she pierced the skin over his clavicle for a central line and glanced at his waxy face. It was Henry. She slipped and hit the artery. A geyser of blood sprayed her, Michael Smith, and the girl who was ventilating with the ambu-bag. When she got the vein, on the third try, she pushed it forward, but his blood clotted even as she pushed it in. "What the hell," she shouted, and there was a pause because they realized, inescapably, after fifteen minutes of flopping his flaccid blue arms, cracking his posthumous ribs, and watching the cardiogram read off an unremittingly straight line, that they were working on a dead man.

"Enough," said Helen. "Get a clean sheet. Wipe up this blood. Get these people out of here."

Michael Smith stood behind her, shaking and weeping, staring at Henry's still face. "His wife," he said, "his children."

"I'm sorry," said Helen.

The narrow hall that led to her room seemed longer than usual and peculiarly dry. She licked her lips, but her tongue stuck to the faint moisture on the roof of her mouth. She thought of calling Henry's wife, getting back to the wards, a memorial service, but the image of a corpse she had once found intruded. It was out in the bush at the end of the dry season, a young boy mauled by a lion so that one arm lay at an unnatural angle, connected only by a tendon that had hardened into rawhide. She stood at her door, looking straight ahead at the eroded slats.

The student, Michael Smith, came up behind her quietly. "Please," he said, touching her arm. She turned slowly and noticed that he was taller than she, how young he was, that his cheeks and nose were freckled with blood, and that he was still weeping.

"What do you want?" she asked him gently, but he just stared at her, moving his hand along her arm. "No," she said, seeing her pale face reflected in his eyes. He reached around her with his other arm and opened the door, pressing against her so she could feel the heat of his body radiating into her own. "Smith," she started, as he bent to kiss her neck. She felt revolted by her wave of desire, sick, like she might vomit. "Go away," she said, "now, before I have to report you to the dean." But when he looked up, his eyes wide and unfocused like a sleepwalker's, she pulled him to her breast and slowly licked the sweat that beaded across his face. "I'm sorry," she whispered. Afterwards, as he lay across her, naked and exhausted, she murmured it again, tracing his lips, "I'm sorry."

"I love you," Smith said, rolling over and going back to sleep, curling defenselessly. Helen stared at him, then got up and showered, letting the water run for hours down her face, between her legs. Then she chose her whitest blouse and went out onto the wards.

"Look," she said to the men's ward secretary. "Has the ward been repainted?"

"No," said the woman.

"But," Helen said in the nursery, "the babies are all so plump and healthy."

"Yes," said the practical nurse who was bathing a new arrival.

Helen walked a long path through the hospital. The women's ward had a new but familiar smell: dust soaked into earth, the beginning of the rainy season.

———————

When she found Diana, she was going over cardiograms with Michael Smith in the emergency room.

"I called Henry's wife," said Diana.

"Yes," said Helen, taking the cardiogram from her, "what's wrong with this patient?"

"Thirty-year-old man with chest pain," began Diana, glancing over at Helen. Michael Smith was looking over Helen's shoulder at the strip of paper. Diana frowned. "Came in this morning," she went on. Michael ran his hand slowly up Helen's thigh. Diana stopped and stared at Helen, at her grey hair, at her grooved cheeks. Helen examined the cardiogram as though nothing had happened.

Diana cleared her throat, her face mottled scarlet. "I understand, Dr. van Horne," she said, "that you've told Mr. Smith he will pass his medicine rotation?"

Helen didn't answer for a moment. "Will you take a fellowship next year?" she asked. "Of course, it is easier to adjust around a husband and children if you work in the emergency room."

"I left my husband," said Diana. "I wanted to be like you."

Helen looked down again at the cardiogram, but her hand began to shake. After a few minutes she said, "And do you think Mr. Smith should pass?"

"No," said Diana.

"Then fail him," said Helen.

"Christ," said Smith to Helen, "that's unfair." When she didn't answer, he looked wounded for a moment, then slammed out of the cubicle.

Diana stared at Helen, embarrassed. "He'll go to the dean," she started.

"Yes," said Helen, "he would be right to do that." She folded the cardiogram carefully back into the chart. She thought of Henry's dead body lying on the gurney waiting for his wife. His lips had turned a particular shade of blue, like the dusky sapphire of Lake Tanganyika at the last moment before the fall of night. It was the most beautiful color she had ever seen.

———

Helen sat on the bed in her room. "I regret to inform you," she wrote to the dean. She stopped and got up, staring at her face in the mirror, overcome with self-disgust. She seemed to herself grotesque, an old woman, a sexual vampire. "Is there ever any justification," she wrote on the wall beside the mirror, "for a teacher—" And yet, the deaths had stopped. She started again, "If A is a middle-aged woman, and B is a young male student, and insects grow, *must* grow in the rotted womb of fallen trees," but she lost interest and turned to the window. Cars honked and revved their engines, beasts of the Serengeti growled and spoke to her. She walked to the window and threw it open, as far as it would go. "It's the rainy season," she shouted to them, "order up the antibiotics, sow the crops." She saw them crowded on the expressway, antelope, giraffe, lions, surrounded by fields of ripened corn. "Yes," she whispered, because she felt at home. She heard the cry of the ambulances, the voices swelling from the emergency room, the beat of the hospital as it trembled with its load of humanity, and for her children, the patients and the students, she obeyed. She spread her arms Daedalus, Icarus, straight at the hot sun of the South Bronx, and hesitated.

Helen climbed down from the windowsill and sat at her desk. "The men," she said firmly, to herself, "do it all the time." She listened for a moment, for a rebuttal. Then she pulled on a white coat, to cover herself, and went out onto the wards.

Brickyard Pond

1

The boy lay floating at the bottom, like he was holding his breath in the bathtub, the way Chris used to when he was a baby. Or so Jerry imagined it. He could see the boy's dark hair radiating out from his head, a black halo absolutely still in the clear water of the abandoned clay pit. Jerry'd heard the old-timers talk about when they used to drain those pits; every so often, they said, turtles and eels and fish would show up flopping on the mud bottom. No one knew how they got there. That's how Jerry understood about the boy; he got there the same way as the other creatures. Immanence. After centuries of habitation, water seeped from the grey-blue Barrington soil so saturated with longing that it precipitated out in the form of this boy.

Not that Jerry'd heard the story direct himself, but his wife Denise grew up just a few blocks from where they lived now, on Maple Avenue. She got it from old Mr. Gaudiani back in the fifties while he was still alive, pruning his grapevines and rocking on the porch. It was one of the boys who fired the donkey-engine that ran from the clay pits to the kilns, a widow's only child from the shack houses where the country club is now. A good boy, hardworking, strong, Mr. Gaudiani said. He figured the boy'd been been down on the beach clamming near where the brick companies' docks were rotted and fallen into the mouth of Mouscachuch Creek, and he'd got caught in bootleggers' crossfire. Then got dumped in one of the flooded pits just to get rid of the body since the federal agents were on their tails.

They certainly couldn't have expected the boy to shine up through the water the next morning the way he did. His radiance startled the clay diggers to the point that, when they saw Maria running at them down the path, they just stepped aside and let her by. It didn't occur to them to shield her, the boy looked so robust, his firm pink arms splayed up like he was reaching for them. And by the time they went to set up the pumps, she was already camped there over her son, cursing and spitting at them in Italian until they gave up and left. As Mr. Gaudiani told the story, he himself was one of the young men who put down his pickaxe and ran to get the pumps. Pump hookups were all over the place; they were fifteen feet below sea level by then, still looking for clay. "Leave him," she shouted in Italian. "Go." She was a sturdy woman of about forty, and she pushed the men away.

For days, said Mr. Gaudiani, weeks, the boy lay suspended in the water, which gave off a kind of cold glow. By winter Crazy Maria had a canvas lean-to and cooked outdoors, shrieking vulgarities at visitors, her matted hair growing out from her head in a fierce bush. When she died, no one but her had been near the pit in years. Soon after that, the clay gave out entirely and the companies went bankrupt. The town flooded the whole area way under and made Brickyard Pond.

The first time Denise told Jerry the story, they were sitting on their bed watching Chris sleep in the bassinette. "I believe the part about the boy drowning," whispered Jerry, "but not the business about him getting shot or staying down looking alive." Jerry was an engineer for Raytheon.

Denise smiled and tiptoed over to Chris. She touched his back with the palm of her hand, feeling for the even rise and fall of his breathing, then turned around and tiptoed back. "Maybe the cold preserved him," she whispered, shrugging her shoulders. "Maybe he wanted to leave Barrington so bad, he just refused to die here."

Every Memorial Day, Denise's family had a barbecue in Veterans Memorial Park alongside the pond, which is how Jerry found out that each member of the family had a different idea of what old Mr. Gaudiani said, and when he said it.

"That was the Altieri boy," said her mother to Jerry, a few years later. "He was killed in the hurricane. Nothing to do with the brickworks at all."

"God," said Denise, rolling her eyes. "You're going to believe her?"

"As I recall," said her father, clearing his throat, "that boy died in the war, Belgium, I think. Anyway," he raised one eyebrow and looked over Denise's head at Jerry, "old Nick Gaudiani never did learn English."

"Come on," laughed Denise, grabbing Jerry's hand. "Let's go wading. You're taking this too seriously."

"You're not supposed to swim there," yelled her brother after them.

"We're not going to *swim*," shouted Denise back. "Watch Chris, will you?" Chris was five now and already wild. "Active," Denise called him, but Jerry watched his curly head disappearing across the stone wall at the end of the street, his legs scrambling up the maple on the corner of their property, his bike charging out into the street, and thought "primordial" was a better word, like a shark or an eel.

Jerry stood with his bare feet in the freezing water, looking out at the marshy island in the middle of the pond and listening to Denise's family. He was an army brat from New York and California and the Philippines. Sometimes it was hard for him to imagine growing up in the same place, all the way through nursing school, the way Denise had. Maybe that was why he married her.

"I believe you," he said to Denise, and he did, slightly revised. The way he saw it, Crazy Maria told her son, over and over, not to swim in the pits, not to go near the bootleggers, not to get caught in the quicksand between the pits and the shore, to look both ways crossing the railroad tracks. But the boy was eighteen and it was a hot night. Maybe he was meeting a girl, maybe just wanting to feel the cool water against his skin. One thing was sure, the boy knew he had to leave. There was no future here, not without clay.

Jerry imagined him floating on his back in the flooded pit, staring up at the stars, listening to the crickets, not wanting to leave, not knowing how to stay. And then the moment of understanding, of transmogrification. The air stills, the boy's heart pauses, it only takes a second, but everything goes slow. He sinks, still floating, down, down. He unlearns breathing and moving, he becomes a water creature, his arms reach up waving gently, an anemone.

"Hey." Jerry turned suddenly to Denise, feeling his chest constrict. "Who's watching Chris?" He looked around and started to run.

"I'm sorry, I'm sorry," apologized Denise's brother after they found Chris playing in the dirt one campground over. "We were playing ball and he just disappeared."

Denise laughed and said, "Little Mr. Independence."

Jerry picked Chris up and put him on his shoulders. "Never," he said, "go where we can't see you. Okay?" Chris squirmed and tried to get down, but Jerry kept his hands firmly around the plump legs until they got back to the rest of the family.

2

Looking at the town now, it was hard to imagine the land was ever wild. Sometimes, walking to the town beach, Jerry and Denise would pass an undeveloped lot tangled with wild grape and ivy. Suddenly the neighboring houses would look like a stage set, like someone moved their living room outdoors, the lawn a wall-to-wall carpet, shrubs for furniture, flowering dogwood for lamps. There was a sense of something lost, underneath, waiting, though it was back even beyond the memories of Denise's grandparents.

That was the way it felt when Jerry knelt in the backyard working in the perennial beds; the foxglove had died out, the columbine was flourishing but had reverted to a pale yellow. The peonies wouldn't bloom at all. But they were there, underneath, it was just a question of the right circumstances. He looked it up in his gardening books. Poor drainage.

Denise came out of the house, wiping her eyes. "For Christ's sake, Jerry," she said, "obsessing about the garden isn't going to solve the problem."

Jerry looked up, lifting his hands out of the earth, where he was working in a layer of builder's sand. Clay soil, the book said, needs something to lighten it up, so air and water can circulate.

"I just can't accept it," she said, sitting down on the back steps and bursting into heaving sobs. "To drop out one semester before the end. One lousy semester."

Jerry came over and sat next to her, holding his arms out in front and trying to brush off the dirt. "Maybe," he said, "you've been working too hard."

Denise had gone back to work, *per diem*; different shifts, different hospitals each week.

The two of them sat there for a moment, listening to the sound of the neighbor's lawnmower, the occasional dog barking, the birds. "I guess," Denise said, after a while, "we won't need the money for tuition any more."

"Denise," said Jerry, "he's not got leukemia, he's not committed any crime. Come on."

"What is he going to do with his life?" shouted Denise. "Live at home and clip people's hedges until he's forty, like my brother? Is that what I chauffeured him here and there for, Little League, soccer, music lessons, RISD art classes, what I wore myself out to pay for B.U. for?"

Jerry went back to working the soil around the peonies.

"You don't even care," said Denise. "You always wanted him to live at home." Jerry sighed. "I wrote him a letter," Denise said, looking past him at the budding rose bushes. "If he wants to stay here he has to pay rent."

"Denise," shouted Jerry, "are you crazy?"

"He's got to grow up." Denise stomped up the stairs into the house. "Theater major, for Christ's sake," she shouted through the screen door. "You couldn't be bothered to encourage him to be an engineer."

Chris's roommate said he'd take a message, but Jerry said no. When he got to Boston, he parked illegally in front of a driveway and ran up into the dorm. The roommate opened the door. Chris's side was empty, the bed stripped, pencils and small bits of things scattered around, the debris of someone just moved out.

"Calm down, Mr. Sullivan," said the boy. Jerry looked at him as if he were watching a movie in slow motion. He was short and neatly dressed, which surprised Jerry. He expected him to be tall and lanky, more like Chris, who had started wearing one gold earring and letting his hair hang in a tangled clump.

"Where is he?" said Jerry.

The boy shrugged his shoulders. "Dunno. Maybe California."

Jerry looked at him in disbelief, then picked up the metal wastebasket and threw it against the wall. It hit with a dull thud. "Hey," said the boy. Jerry went out and slammed the door.

"Listen," the boy called down the hall, "it's okay. He just needed to go, you understand?"

3

By August it was clear that Chris wasn't going to write, although in June they'd gotten a postcard of San Diego with "Don't worry Got a job washing boats Will write soon," scrawled across the back in his unmistakable messy handwriting.

At first, Jerry would sit in Chris's room, on the bed, just looking at the U2 posters on the wall, the junior-high team pictures, the fourth-grade scholastic achievement award. Sometimes, Denise came in and perched awkwardly next to him on the side of the bed, her anger spilling out into the silence. They'd been through it over and over again. Jerry was worn out from hypotheses. He could feel the room drying up, stiffening, and he was beginning to have trouble breathing.

Allergies, said Denise, dust, but Jerry knew it was the emptiness in the house, hardening around him like an exoskeleton.

On Labor Day, Denise's parents invited them for a picnic at Colt State Park, down in Bristol. Denise was spending more and more time with her parents. They needed her, she told Jerry, it was getting hard for them to do things for themselves. Denise's brother tried to start up a game of softball, but nobody really wanted to play. Denise and her mother were talking about living room furniture. "Why don't you get some really nice pieces," her mother said. "That's what your father and I did at your stage of life."

Jerry was helping himself to potato salad, but he looked up when Denise's mother said that. Without Chris, she meant. Just the two of us. He suddenly saw Denise, how tired she looked, how her face was grooved, and her mother's heavy maroon velvet curtains, the gold brocade couch, the hard wing chair. He felt a wave of tenderness toward her. "Neecie," he thought, "Neecie," mentally stroking her hair, tucking it behind her ear.

He got up and walked down to the edge of the water. He could see all the way across to the houses on Warwick Neck, their land running down to the water like the house Denise had once refused to buy. She'd been pregnant with their second child, before they knew what a miracle Chris had been, before she started with the miscarriages. Jerry found a bigger house, a Colonial on Hundred Acre Cove. She was excited by the size of it, the family room, the fireplace, the view. Then, as she went out in the backyard, Chris broke away from her and ran right past the old swing set and into the rushes by the water. Startled for a moment, they watched his shoulders disappear into the high sea grass. "No," she said, when they got back to the realtor, who was waiting by the deck. "No." Jerry didn't argue. As it turned out, they didn't need a bigger house anyway.

Jerry walked over to the picnic table and put his arms around Denise. Her parents were packing the car, arguing about how to fold the plastic table cloth. "Neecie," he said softly, "why don't you quit nursing and go back to school? Isn't that what you always wanted to do?" He could feel her tense up, then she burst suddenly into tears. "What's the matter?" he asked. "Did I say something wrong?"

"No," she said, wiping her eyes with the back of her hand. But she wouldn't look at him. After a while, Jerry left to help her parents.

That night they lay next to each other in bed and, just before she fell asleep, Denise reached over to touch his face. "Jerry," she said, enunciating slowly, as if she was talking through a window or under water, "I love you."

Jerry lay for a while, listening to the rhythm of her breathing and the small creaks and rustles of the house around them. Then he slid out of bed and went into the kitchen, where the moonlight glanced across the dishes he'd stacked in the rack to dry. It had always been Chris's job to put them away; sometimes Jerry still left them, out of habit. Jerry began to put them away, but he was too restless to stand still. He went back into the bedroom and got dressed, quickly, furtively. The backyard floated dimly through the kitchen window. The peonies glistened as he passed them, and he brushed their leaves with his hand.

When he got to Maple Avenue, he started toward the park at a slow jog. The deserted street looked familiar but different, like a close friend he hadn't seen in years. In the windows of the Vienna Bakery a pale middle-aged man stared back at him through the empty display cases, and he realized with a shock that it was his own face he saw. He began to run faster, down West Street, across the bicycle path and past the Y. He felt released, burst out of something, like he'd been holding his breath. When he finally saw the pond, he slowed down, panting. The black water reflected the moon, except in the ripples it looked perfectly round, but in the sky he could tell that it was really just past fullness, already slightly asymmetric. Jerry sat down on a rock and rubbed his eyes. For the first time in what seemed like years he felt fully awake. He looked around at the shadowy trees, the silent campgrounds. How he would miss this place. The thought hurt, as if he were already gone, longing to return. He stood up and paced on the muddy pine needles, closing his eyes. He tried to imagine Indians feasting here, farmers, brickyards, even the boy just under the surface of the pond, but he couldn't, not for more than a few seconds. There was an excitement flowing into him, up from the soil, like sap—he thought about the Philippines, Central America, maybe China. He felt pared down, ready to move again. An engineer could be useful. He imagined himself efficient, solitary, free.

Suddenly the park closed in, clotting his airways, like he was drowning. Whatever had held them together, made them a family, was running out. And he didn't know how to make it stay. Far out on the pond, a fish slapped against the water. Jerry listened, then sank back into the rock. He slowed his breathing, trying to relax. Then he waited for the moment of understanding, of precipitation. *Father. Husband.* He waited to unlearn.

My German
Problem

I was the American girl righteousness rolled off me
a mighty stream I rose from my desk Peter Pan collar angel wings
looked Frl. Weisskopf in the eye hated them all and said I have nothing to say. Oh I'd been there a month or so—it was the nippy end of
September art class and I had it figured out. My father said everything began with Sarajevo, well maybe with Versailles but he was
a man. Any girlchild could see those black-and-white photos Anne
Frank her shiny parted hair how it all started with lies parents children
teachers students ganging up betraying each other I was pretty sure
of this and fed up. Fourteen is a fierce uncharitable age even though
I was raised Berkeley California NAACP ACLU agnostic WASP into
the religion of understanding: my sister off to the Peace Corps my

brother voter registration my father back and forth across Europe for nuclear disarmament with my mother tagged along smiling (those were the times). Which is how I'd gotten into this fix in the first place: What an opportunity, my mother said, Really get to know another culture and they stuck me in a German boarding school and left me there.

Frl. Weisskopf struck like a snake, ruler across my wrist a rising welt. I was used to it by now, the girls laughing behind her back, spitballs on the ceiling timed to drop, Pigface on the blackboard, ink blots on her notes, then when she came in all stand up polite as can be GOOD MORNING FRL. DIREKTOR WEISSKOPF. She with her rules and her belt and her ruler and they all fall over themselves to rat first. We came to Germany by way of Washington that summer I heard King at the Lincoln Memorial, *this nation will rise up and live out the true meaning of its creed . . .* actually I read it later the sound system wasn't good but I understood the truth the beauty of it even though I was too young to really know what it was I was understanding.

So I looked out the window at the last blowsy roses of summer occasional seed on the black Bavarian soil and from the serenity of my parents' green American rocket car I turned to the class and said: I can't condone being so mean to someone who never did anything to you. Ursel sat twisting the sign she'd torn off her back (I'm a Fat SS Whoredaughter) smiling a little hate smile at me. I looked at the teacher her eyes popping out and went on, But it's up to them I don't think it's right to tattle. Weisskopf roared boxed my ears until they rang but justice and freedom rang louder and I sat down red-faced, trembling and so satisfied I could float away.

It should have ended there but Ursel had something to say. Don't concern yourself, she called across the room the whispering died down: She *was* an SS whore but my father was American at least his boots were that's all she could see. URSEL shouted Frl. Weisskopf a high flush across her slavic cheeks THAT IS ENOUGH and she pulled Ursel up by her ear and marched her out of the room. Hypocrites, said Ursel on her way out the door. At least *they* had some German pride. Weisskopf slapped her so hard she fell against the door.

They hated her, pudgy pale Catholic, older than the rest, always around even during vacations, pictures of JFK and the Pope taped to her bed, but everyone, even the Protestant popularity queen who'd done it, came over to the empty desk to see what she'd been working on. We were doing *Erlkönig* that month and Ursel could draw. A horse leapt elongated Chagall carrying the father his cradled son over elms sticking up like hairbrushes in the mist of the moon. So tender the father his love his rush his rescue, we stared trapped we touched our fingertips charcoal darkened our boarding school dreams our visitless days our middle-of-the-night longings. And *she* had drawn it. On the top Ursel had written: *In seinen Armen das Kind war tot.* In that moment I loved her hated her too struck mute would have been her slave.

We were still crowded around staring when Ursel came back sullen following the assistant art teacher we scattered back to our seats. Weisskopf came in a few minutes later without looking up began going down the rows grading papers. She gave out a few Fs and Ds but when she got to Ursel's she stopped frozen cleared her throat. Ursel turned and looked out the window I wished with sudden anger I could draw, sing, anything I felt so far from McDonald's the flat wide asphalt of home.

So, said Weisskopf when she got to me, Don't they teach anything in the U.S.A.? She grabbed my hand with the pencil, smelled of marzipan and wool her heavy silver ring tore my fingers, she bent me to the lines: a good solid horse, a tail, a mane, strong legs running. Make it beautiful, she whispered. I cried out but she ignored me. Her horse was better than mine.

It was sometime after I noticed how carefully Frl. Direktor Weisskopf tended the rose garden in front of the school. Pruned back for winter the yellow briers, damasks, moss, climbers, the floribundas, hybrid teas, polyanthas clipped neatly mulched in clusters. Crimson, apricot, pink gone now the brambles revealed a structural geometry of paths and roses, concentric circles. She worked late into fall snipping here there bleeding on the thorns bundling the most tender into burlap. I watched alone, scuffling the gravel during recess. Weeks went by, no one ever spoke of it again, Ursel's mother, the SS, the war. I was German enough by now I didn't bring it up let it lie coiled under every glance every laugh I didn't care just wondered why they didn't like me worried about my thighs and counted the days until Christmas. Ursel never spoke to me at all.

School went on, into the showers five thirty in the morning wet naked embarrassed for inspection our hard-nippled adolescent breasts did you use soap? our sprouting pubic hair some teachers turned away the fat old ones always looked. Then study half an hour seven A.M. line up in front of the life-size wooden Jesus nailed blood drops to the cross in the dining hall with three part Bach chorals. By the time we settled on the long plastic-covered tables for tea and bread the pumpernickel was already stolen by the girls who stood in the back. But there was always *bauernbrot.* I smeared it with butter bit through the crust, slid it around my mouth closed my eyes to taste better and got through the day until I could hide private under my feather bed imagining dry hills valley oaks a hot summer day drinking root beer drift off to sleep dreams of home.

When my parents took me away for Christmas the only thing I asked for was a radio. Why? said my father disapproving because they'd already got my gift. How could I explain November the girls rushing *attentat* whispering *attentat* shocked looking at me I didn't understand the word finally Ursel reached into her bedside table a tiny transistor radio pulled out the earplug and I understood. Kennedy. Ursel threw herself sobbing on the bed we all looked at his picture over her head so young vital and I heard American underneath the German translating I heard my language rolling round relaxed soft even in disaster it had been so long like a memory of mother holding me clean and warm from the bath. One of the girls shouted, How could you kill him? I looked at her said, What? but Ursel sat up slowly and said, Because he was Catholic because he was good. She turned the dial and threw the radio at me. Here, she shouted, it's your country you listen. And a flood of American came at me full familiar no German over it at all. Army station said Ursel because I must have looked stunned I had no idea I guess I hadn't thought about all those Americans so nearby. They were talking bullets shattered head and blood communists negro civil rights hate, they were crying on the air I was crying too but I was listening to the words the sounds oh god how I loved my language my tongue my home no matter what they said in it and I was ashamed. Ursel watched me with a bitter smile but didn't say anything and after a while she took it and changed the channel back to German.

Please let me stay home, I said to my father we were driving away from the school. Please. Now come on, said my mother, We've been through all that it's always hard at first you'll get used to it. I'll never get used to it, I cried, it's so lonely. I didn't want to cry but I was desperate. That's enough, said my father. If I just had a radio, I begged, transistor a little one.

Isn't that against the rules? said my mother. Mom, I said, I sobbed I pleaded. The headmistress, what's her name? started my mother, Weisskopf, I muttered. Came running out, she went on, that woman *is* built like a hun isn't she, anyway she told us not to park the car where the other girls could see and not to come with so many packages. Not fair to the others, you know. Called the car a *strassenkreutzer*, laughed my father. Don't you just love the German language? I looked at my father and suddenly saw him how his hands trembled when he talked to repair men, how my mother smoothed her skirts, how they both smiled when they talked to the border guards the headmistress the police. I felt sick. They didn't get me a radio.

For Christmas we went to Italy. On the train I thought about Weisskopf telling them to move the car how rich I must seem to them the worn shoes the patched jackets in my misery I hadn't noticed even Weisskopf herself was probably poor. I had noticed Ursel watching as we pulled away she spent a lot of time at the window of the solarium I think she was working on the *Erlkönig* a city version the horse floating over rooftops and chimneys the moonlight spreading out over Munich glancing off the Cathedral touching lovers by the Isar and casting a halo around the German Museum.

All the way through Siena that black-and-white cathedral Florence squares bridges the Uffizi Rome following my mother's guidebook Saint Peter's I felt guilty: Ursel should be seeing this, how Ursel would enjoy that. Rich piggish American guilty. I suppose it was this feeling building up that finally exploded in front of Michelangelo's *Pietà* looking at the drape of the Madonna's veil her stern face her dead and punctured child me trying to figure out the inscription on her sash suddenly I knew Ursel was a great artist those California suburban lessons wasted on me I had so much but no one ever visited her and in a great rush of feeling I said to my mother: There's a girl in our school who's really good at drawing but can't afford private lessons.

When we got back my parents offered Weisskopf to pay for Ursel's lessons I knew they would it was their kind of thing, or at least I was pretty sure they did because the first thing Ursel did when she saw me walk into the solarium was throw a bag of art supplies at my feet.

I stood still watching the brushes the pastels the little bottles of oils roll around on the floor. I hadn't noticed Weisskopf in the corner but she stood up with dignity and said, Ursel you will apologize. They stared at each other some kind of private war then Ursel turned to me hissed, Sorry, with a look like an ice pick and ran out of the room. Weisskopf bent down slowly gathered up the art supplies when she finished said, She needs the lessons it was kind . . . but she couldn't finish her face flushed as if she were angry her eyes teared up she left the room. Afterwards I thought maybe I just imagined the tears because it wasn't like her and none of the other girls said anything at all, just went on reading their magazines, combing each other's hair as if nothing had happened. I sat on the couch next to a girl in fifth form she got up and moved somewhere else so I opened up a letter from a friend at Berkeley High. Sorry it's been so long, she wrote, My mother nags my father lectures my sister's a brat god you're so lucky you don't have to live at home bet you're having a blast. Went to a party last night you should see who's popular now when you come back won't even know them a whole different crowd.

I should have left Ursel alone but I couldn't help myself I felt the generosity flowing through my veins humble beneficence from my fingertips I smiled kindly at her in class offered to do her kitchen duty after lunch in art Weisskopf announced Ursel was leaving for tutoring the other girls snickered I floated godliness she packed her satchel pulled on her sweater from the back of the room someone whispered bye-bye honey in English but she left the room without turning around.

When she came back she was changed jumpy plugged in charged up full of life. She showed everyone her new books talked nervous jerky frantic on and on about the tutor sketched the whole class from different perspectives then started in on each girl alone. They were quiet watching her waiting a garden in winter but I spoke right up said: I wish I could draw like that Ursel. There was silence. She looked at me blank then suddenly threw the paper the pastels the tissue in her desk closed it with a bang. Someone started to hum it was a little German tune they were laughing at me it's o.k. I told myself and turned the other cheek.

But it was a long dragged day couldn't float forever on holiness here I was back in prison no visits until Easter lonely foreign by dinnertime kept blinking back the tears. In the bathroom brushing teeth everyone telling everyone else what they did over vacation no one asked me at all so I sprinkled the powder on my toothbrush scrubbed back and forth wiped a washcloth across my face smiled for inspection and ran back into the sleeping hall trying not to cry. It was odd quiet in the hall even though half the girls were there expectant and watching I didn't really notice hit so heavy with homesickness this was the worst ever that hammer that emptiness go in a corner and moan missing home so much hallucinating California eucalyptus smells hot dust fog hamburgers and Tussy cinnamon deodorant I wanted to leap into sleep dream forever. Almost lights-out I was about to turn my bed was at the end left I heard Hssst coming from the other end right.

It was Ursel. She held up her radio, twisted it invitingly and smiled. I looked at her looked back at my piled high feather bed my stuffed Pekinese bedtable greeting cards, letters, old bits of home I wanted to go private hiding alone but something turned me looked back at Ursel again. The radio was off I heard it anyway rock and roll those American sounds pulled me tugged me sucked like a tar pit she smiled her SS teeth saber teeth I was caught the more I struggled the more I knew I had to have that radio it was against the rules I didn't care it was home she wanted me to beg oh she knew just how much I wanted it this was her revenge.

I pulled myself together walked slowly down to her bed tried to act nonchalant shouldn't assume she's up to anything maybe she wants to be friends two outcasts besides it's not fair to think SS just because some rumor about her mother I remembered later that September time after class a day-student pulled me aside she had braided blond hair a high clear forehead she was upset she said, My parents will take you to visit Dachau it's quite near don't think we've all swept it under the rug these girls just feel sorry for them their parents don't want them, nicht? At the time I didn't know what to make of it all but I could see it wasn't fair to judge someone by their parents.

So I walked up to Ursel smiled my eyes on the radio she turned on the station oh I twisted I writhed How're you all out there in radio land? said the announcer I heard him home home home. I reached and Ursel pulled the radio back a little. Hey it's a meeting of the fat thigh society, yelled Miss Popularity and the suck-up girls all laughed. Ursel, I said and I saw the triumph in her eyes, Please. Hola SS Ursel, yelled another, Maybe you found your U.S. sister. Ursel ignored them all just kept her eyes on mine moving the radio slowly back so I had to lunge for it I did grabbed fell across her dressing table and gashed my nose it bled. She laughed. You want it don't you, she whispered, you want it more than anything else in the world. I looked at her in pain and nodded. Then say Thank you Ursel, she shouted. I reached again and felt the hard plastic case in my hand clutched it slid it under my bathrobe never letting go Thank you Ursel, I said the blood was streaming down my face humiliated but I had it now rock and roll coming from my belly I clicked it off secret can't risk losing it now turned toward my bed and ran. But not soon enough.

We all heard that clump clump clump down the stairs it could be only one thing: Weisskopf coming to put out the lights. My heart began to race I felt my knees tremble I was a good girl not experienced at breaking rules I panicked. She was coming closer my legs took over of themselves fired me right into the bed nearest the door past the girl I didn't know her well except she was Catholic her mouth puckered in surprise I dive-burrowed down under the covers by her feet. And I curled there safe dark womb without breathing.

WHERE IS THE AMERICAN Weisskopf's voice boomed through the comforter. Then there was a silence. Suddenly she yelled again. MARIA WHAT IS THAT LUMP IN YOUR BED? Cold ripped into the glaring light from my sanctuary she whipped off the covers grabbed my arm threw me on the floor the radio fell out of my hand slid across the linoleum landed right at her feet. So she said. I was terrified stared at her white wool socks heavy black orthopedic shoes couldn't think just started to shake sweat caught cornered run to the ground.

What are you doing out of your bed, said Weisskopf I looked at her dumb she stared at me I couldn't speak BY GOD YOU WILL SPEAK she shouted and she grabbed me by the hair and pulled me to a kneel I looked up saw Ursel. Jolted me into consciousness her eyes satisfied waiting she knew I would tell on her now I saw they were all just waiting. I felt a hardening inside something that wasn't afraid growing knifing up green through the ice primeval remorseless stubborn. I said nothing. Weisskopf held my eyes in hers and started pulling off her belt. Maria, she said, what was this girl doing in your bed?

I don't know, whispered Maria. Whose radio is it Maria? Weisskopf was still looking at me her hard black eyes no expression but underneath there was excitement. She was enjoying this. I felt hate a warm succoring firm rush of hate. Not mine, said Maria her voice cracked I could sense her trembling I never noticed her much before there were several Marias confused them all. TELL ME barked Weisskopf at me OR I WILL BE FORCED TO PUNISH BOTH OF YOU. I looked at her and at Ursel, at her waiting longing eyes she wanted this strapping herself she wanted to kneel to hurt it was hers to hate be hated I stared at her decided with my gut not even thinking just looked at her and knew what I had to do sweat running down my sides words stuck in my throat but I croaked it out THE RADIO IS MINE.

Weisskopf stared at me. And what were you doing in Maria's bed? Are you one of those nasty girls who like other girls? I wasn't doing anything, I said. If you don't tell me . . . she said softly clearly. No, cried Maria, It was her and Ursel. Nothing to do with me at all. Is that true? said Weisskopf. I didn't answer. Ursel? she said. Ursel said nothing she was waiting for me to name her point to her betray her I looked back and forth Weisskopf hard little eyes high cheekbones Ursel raisin eyes pudgy face cheekbones something was bothering me back of my mind but it vanished Weisskopf was in a rage now. YOU WILL STAY HERE EASTER YOU TOO MARIA she shouted I heard Maria behind me whispering, Oh God No. You are all the same, Weisskopf screamed, lying girls so lazy when I was a girl worked too hard to cause any trouble at night but YOU she stared at me YOUR parents buy you this that anything you want spoiled silly you won't bring your radio your ignorant American ways into my school. Please, said Maria, I want to see my *mutti*, I didn't do anything. So? said Weisskopf looking at me and I was hearing Maria crying *mutti mutti* and looking at Ursel's pale Bavarian face and Weisskopf's pale Bavarian face back and forth and I suddenly realized what had been bothering me before. Now I knew. Mother daughter Weisskopf Ursel I knew it for sure.

I must have stared because Weisskopf paused I looked around the room. Ursel gave me a little grimace of spite and Weisskopf abruptly shrieked So? again I looked at her face and a will rose up in me I would not be bullied I would not tattle I was an American girl I stared no no no at Weisskopf and she was in a fury, reached down tore off my nightgown I was naked in front of all of them heart shaking the sudden violence of it the air on my breasts. I had hair around my nipples they were looking my body exposed oh god I grabbed the nightgown to cover my front pain shot across my back she was lashing me with the belt stinging burning each whip rushed through my body faint I thought I would pass out. I looked up at Ursel she was angry she hadn't wanted it to turn out this way the belt came again I screamed couldn't help myself in front of all of them she humbled me my naked buttocks bent over they could even see my crotch oh the pain them all quiet watching I could hear Maria praying the Lord's Prayer *Our Father* I saw the patterned linoleum as if from a great distance all I knew was pain would have done anything to stop the pain I was a beast screaming no mind no thoughts just pain. She was coming faster and faster out of control suddenly I felt a blow hurt lost my breath she kicked me in the ribs and left the room.

I lay numb curled on the floor for a minute then the throbbing began I tried to straighten up pain I raised my head looked at Ursel I was broken a naked beast in front of all of them but I knew and she knew it. I looked in her eyes saw nothing but black like the window behind her darkness reaching out across the city roofs chimneys everywhere I looked away. The girl Maria crouched beside me and smeared something cold on my back I cried out but after a minute the pain got less she wrapped a towel around my chest still crying herself Here she said and I saw she meant for me to raise my arms like a child she dressed me covered me my nightgown I looked away from her I'm sorry I said sick repulsed by myself what I had done to her my pride my anger. She didn't answer I looked up again this German girl Maria almost a stranger she looked at me with pity. I crawled back to my bed.

By Easter time I didn't care much that my parents weren't taking me away things didn't seem so urgently awful anymore. I spoke German without an accent even *Grüss Gott* Bavarian with the rest of them shopkeepers couldn't tell the difference. I was one of the group walked round and round the rose garden just blooming new tender yellows and pinks sweetest smell on earth arm in arm with the Protestant girls telling me how to dress Catholic girls trying to convert me. Traded off going to church Catholic Protestant but in the end Catholic won because they had Thursdays best pastry shop in Munich on the way to confession they made little chocolate-covered marshmallow things *Mohrenköpfen* kind of chocolate Mallomars became so fond of those I told Weisskopf I'd suffered a sudden illumination and from then on I was Catholic. Ursel changed too. Didn't seem to care about me anymore just kept quiet to herself drawing sleeping and losing weight not talking to anyone not even listening to her radio.

Vacation came the other girls went away with their parents waves goodbyes bustling packing promises to write bring gifts and left me and Maria and Ursel alone. Maria sobbed for her mother her father I felt remorse grab me squeeze my neck Ursel paid no attention at all. A couple days later Ursel left too. One of the Third Form teachers came solemn the next day into the solarium sat down on the couch and said to Maria and me, Ursel is in the hospital. Maria stopped sniffling for a minute and looked up red eyes the teacher said, Doctor said she's getting too thin don't know what's wrong. I waited wasn't sure what I was supposed to say. The teacher looked at me hesitated looked down said, We thought maybe someone her own age visiting a friend. Maria and I looked at each other. I'm not sure I said. No, said Maria. The teacher didn't move I saw the drawings filling the wastebasket the charcoal still on the table the horse the rider over and over I looked out the window to the darkening sky a spring storm coming and I said, Yes. I'll go. But I don't think she'll want to see me.

Ursel was sitting up skeletal in the bed yellow skin against the rough white sheets turned her head away when I came in. Weisskopf stood up motioned me outside came out closed the door. It was the first time she'd really spoken to me since the beating. She looked at me. They think, she said, maybe she's unhappy lonely can't find anything else wrong. I'm sorry, I said, and I really was even though she was foreign to me now and I wasn't sure at all what she was feeling. Maybe you can talk to her? she said. Frl. Direktor Weisskopf, I said, Ursel doesn't like me she doesn't want to see me. Weisskopf looked at me angry. Listen, I said, still fourteen not knowing when to shut up, It's hard for her they make fun of her she doesn't have parents like the others . . . Go away said Weisskopf. You Americans will never understand you are not capable of it.

When I got back to the school the wind was rising and it was raining sleeting getting cold. I went inside and found Maria sitting in the study hall her head down on the desk. Maria, I said. I'm sorry I never meant it please forgive me I need you to forgive me. She didn't answer but after a while she put her arms around my shoulders and I hugged her too we sat there a long time just holding each other thinking in the stillness of the empty school.

Let's walk, said Maria looking out the window, before it turns dark the storm's over I'm sick of being inside. I stood up light was coming in slanting through the windows rays of suspended dust hanging in the air always there but suddenly apparent and we walked arm in arm through the dining hall past the wooden Jesus his skinny ribs out the entrance hall and blinked at the cold sun. Maybe it was our eyes weren't adjusted or maybe it was the clarity of the ice but it took us a minute to realize what had happened to the roses. An ice storm, cried Maria and ran to touch the frozen blossoms glittering crystal swaying in the soft wind. Hush, I said and we listened there was a tinkling like a thousand pieces of broken glass rustling in the breeze. Oh, said Maria and she ran inside to bring the teachers. I stood never seen anything so beautiful these ice roses sparkling against the blue sky even the thorns glistened with artefact I looked around circle after circle her precious roses the delicacy the colors the fragility suddenly I felt frightened there was no smell no softness no life it was beautiful beyond compare it was dead dead dead. I turned walked ran suffocated through the rows wanted to get away anywhere rushed past the teachers coming out their cries of astonishment pleasure tore up the stairs into the sleep hall threw myself on the bed buried my head under the pillow.

That night after everyone was asleep I got up tiptoed down the empty hall to the solarium and sat looking out the window I knew the year was almost over and I was going home. I looked out the moon hung a flat coin against the clouds the city glowed black and white roofs chimneys more chimneys than I'd ever seen before rising thin like blades of silver grass into the night I looked sleepy blinked my eyes. For a minute I saw Ursel's horse leaping out across the roofs the rider the child suspended motionless I knew her shiny parted hair it was a girlchild lying so still in his arms. I blinked again and it was gone. I sat there for a while on the couch couldn't sleep so I pulled my brother's letter from my pocket and read it again just to feel it touch it safe home. Dear Tootsie Roll, he wrote, school drags on but I'm about to do something real signed up to go down into the deep South this summer it's exciting going to work for CORE start a Freedom School teach the kids their rights register the adults. It's a good thing little sister feels right lots of us going I just don't understand those people down there I mean can't they see how wrong it is the way they're behaving telling lies acting as if nobody mattered but themselves? The letter went on but I folded it stroked it looked up at the moon its crystal light spilling down silvering my hand the paper the roofs the chimneys spreading out glittering over Munich yes over the parks the halls the museums past the city limits a jeweled net streaming over Germany reaching out beautiful glinting towards my brother towards home.

Ambulance

I was putting my feet up with the evening shift nurse on the women's ward. Marie was a practical nurse; this was the old Lincoln Hospital in the south Bronx, and the city only paid for registered nurses on the day shift. Not that the patients weren't in completely capable hands with Marie. She was a sharp Jamaican duststorm of a woman, tiny, wiry, and astoundingly energetic. Most evenings, the ward hopped like a nightclub with one demented act; she sang, she scolded, she exhorted, she divulged. She was an efficient pied piper, sucking those sick people right out of themselves, away from broken linoleum and army-green cloth partitions and the disinfected stench of the open ward. On Marie's shift, the junkies were so entertained they even gave up their usual pastime of knocking the roaches off the curtains.

Anyway, that evening things were quiet on the ward. Marie and I had finished the chores, tucked everyone in, and sat down to rest our feet and talk. I was sweating in the heat of the New York night, but she was starchy and crisp as usual. Marie's voice was as quick and precise as her body. She spoke in a patois recitative, accompanied by the whirr of the fan, the flies buzzing, and the chanting. Always the chanting. Marie called them her singers, the ones who went to their death not groaning, not screaming, but singing, coaxing death with a monody of "gates, gates, gates in the sky," or "wash the baby, the baby, Oh Lord, the baby," or "cooking, scrubbing, cooking, scrubbing." The three old women were placed one on each end of the ward and one in the middle. Marie always prepared them for the night by smoothing their pillows and straightening their sheets, as if they were still aware. And they just kept on crooning their way into death, putting the rest of us to sleep.

Marie was talking about her son. "That one, my Jamey, he's a smart one." She laughed. "He put himself in law school, oh my. He's gonna be something. He always was a crackerjack."

"Is he married?"

"Oh sure, and the first little one on the way. Imagine me a grandmama."

"Marie, don't you have another son?"

"Yeah honey, I do."

"What does he do?"

"I don't know. I haven't seen him now, two years it will be. I lost him young." She sat absolutely still.

"Lost him to what, if you don't mind my asking?"

"Lost him to the streets. Jamey, though, now you should have seen him in high school. Wasn't he the sharp one!" and she was moving again.

There was a tendency in the south Bronx to describe the place as a living thing, a sort of monster, a filthy maw of burned-out buildings that chewed up children and spat them out broken, lost. I didn't ask any more about the other son.

In that silence, the paging began. It started innocently. Just the chief of the emergency room wanted for an emergency. Nothing much to wonder about. Then the senior house surgeon to the emergency room. Then the security personnel to the emergency room. Then all the senior doctors still in the hospital to the emergency room.

Then, "All doctors to the emergency room, stat, all doctors to the emergency room, stat." The page operator spoke with a peculiar nasal urgency.

I jumped off my chair and looked at Marie.

"Not you, honey, you're a medical student."

"But what's going on down there?"

"Whatever it is, you best stay here. You'll be the only kind of doctor we got up here now." She readjusted her legs on the chair.

Then the page sounded again, "All medical students to the emergency room, stat, all medical students to the emergency room, stat."

This time I tore down the hall, my short white coat flying. There was no safe place to leave things at Lincoln, so when you came for overnight duty, you brought everything in your pockets. All medical students bulged with the tuberous accretions of their status. Coins, notebooks, ophthalmoscope, pens, syringes, and tampax came jumping out of my pockets as I rounded the stairwell. I clutched my pockets and tried to glide. As I came down the last hall, I could hear the emergency room. Something was definitely going on there. Solo yells and screams peaked over a general chaotic chorus, like some experimental war requiem. I charged into the waiting room and stopped dead.

The strict rows of wooden chairs had been overturned, kicked out of the way. The middle of the room was a twitching mass of muscle and skin, with a pause provided here and there by a knife blade, a chain, an ice pick. I had seen knife fights in the waiting room before, but the scale of this one was staggering. There must have been fifty kids in studded leather jackets going at each other. Several policemen were clubbing with staccato bashes. In the corner, an isolated security guard was wrenching a gun from a boy. The boy's jacket had "Death Lords" spelled across the back in a rhinestone arc. On the floor were two clumps of doctors and nurses trying to resuscitate bleeding bodies. Oblivious to the chaos around them, they were moving through their routines; pumping chests, starting intravenous lines, calling to each other.

The audience to all this was the arriving relatives and girl friends, some in torn jeans, some in cheap but businesslike suits, some dressed for a night on the town. They were crying and reaching from the sidelines; now and then a woman's high wail sang out as she saw a son fall. The girls were paired on the floor, their spike heels and ankle chains coiled in vicious duos, green nails ripping faces as they tried to unroot each other's acrylic hair.

I stood paralyzed by the entrance. One of the guards spotted me there and forcefully gesticulated that I should go across the waiting room and into the treatment area of the emergency room. Without thinking, I plunged through the spectacle and found myself in the treatment area.

Here, things were much the same, except that there were more bodies lying flat with people working on them, and fewer still upright, causing damage.

"Here, hold this!" A surgical intern pushed my hand over a man's neck. I let the pressure slack a second while I stepped closer. A hot shower of blood sprayed over me, soaking into my whites, splattering my face. I pushed harder and it stopped. I angled around the other people cutting and stitching and pumping and breathing, and managed to wipe my glasses. Out of the corner of my eye, I saw the knife coming and stepped aside as a pale boy with a bloodstained T-shirt erupted through the crowd.

"Gonna finish the job, you son-of-a-bitch!" He staggered back. Somebody tripped him; he fell on the tile floor and didn't get up again.

An arm brushed my shoulder. I turned with a jump to see the chief resident on duty that night. He was shouting something at me. I grabbed a nearby hand and pressed it on the neck wound, then followed the chief.

He shouted, "Medical student?"

I nodded.

"Need you to ride an ambulance. Supposed to send an M.D., but we can't spare any. You'll have to go. Go out to the bay, we'll bring the patient."

The night air was a shock—dark, cool, and quiet. An ambulance sat there, back doors open, ready to receive. The driver leaned out, an unremarkable man. He pulled the pipe out of his mouth.

"You the doc?"

"Yes."

He nodded contentedly and disappeared again into the dark.

"Hey, medical student!" Two emergency room nurses were wheeling out a stretcher. A still form lay on it, gleaming in the night. I walked over.

"Here's the papers, you'll have to bag him." She handed me the bag. I had never used one before. I squeezed it as she had, forcing the air down the tube into his lungs. She turned to walk away.

"But where are we going and what am I supposed to do?"

"Keep him alive if you can." She turned back into the emergency room.

By this time, the other nurse and an orderly had lifted the stretcher into the ambulance and rolled the patient onto the narrow cot attached to one side. I was moving with them, trying to squeeze the bag in a kind of breathing-dance. I had never paid much attention to breathing before.

They closed the doors and I was alone in the back. In the dim light of the emergency lamp, the frail papers of the temporary chart were almost unreadable. Slowly I made out the writing. He was "unknown male," and we were going to Jacobi Hospital for neurosurgery. He had a bullet in his head.

I looked down at him. He was eighteen or twenty, motionless aside from my breathing. His face was serene, as if lost in the deep sleep of childhood. There, frozen forever, the sweet four year old, the clever eight year old, the awkward twelve year old. The top of his head was bandaged, but there was no other mark on the smooth skin of his body. I wondered what his name was.

The ambulance started, the siren went on with a deafening wail, and we shot out of the hospital bay. The violence of the ride surprised me; I was barely able to keep my balance as we swung onto the Bronx River Parkway. I did my best to keep squeezing the bag as we swerved through the dense traffic, but I was frightened. The light inside the ambulance flickered with each maneuver, as if with a faulty connection. As we roared shrieking off the Parkway and onto Fordham Road, disaster struck. A car cut in front of us, and the ambulance driver veered suddenly, accelerating around it. I went flying across the back and landed with a crack against the glass of the rear doors. I wasn't looking, but I saw it anyway, the Bronx River churning in the moonlight below the doors. The water foamed ominously over fierce rocks, figments of the dimming moon. I turned to look for the boy (I called him Angelo). He had slid off his cot and onto the floor, sprinkled with nickels and dimes from my coat. Underneath the glitter he was turning dusky blue.

I screamed for the driver, but nothing could be heard over the noise of the siren. We were hurtling relentlessly toward Jacobi. Panicked, I straightened his body and smoothed the pillow under his head.

I forced a sudden, rational calm. Think. You can reason this out. He's turning blue because he doesn't have enough air. Give him air. I tried to squeeze the bag harder. Nothing moved. So. The tube is blocked. I looked at the tube. It had been pulled out when he fell, and the end was stuck in his mouth. If the tube isn't in the lungs, the air isn't going there. How am I going to get air to his lungs? Oh Angelo, stay alive. Mouth-to-mouth resuscitation. I'll just keep it up until we get there. I yanked the tube completely out and pulled back his jaw. We were still sliding back and forth along the floor of the ambulance as it jerked and turned, accelerated and stopped. OK. I learned this. I can do this. I did it.

I didn't notice that we were there until they opened the back doors, flooding the ambulance with the neon lights of Jacobi's emergency room. The light hurt my eyes, and I didn't dare stop breathing. I just stayed where I was, breathing into Angelo's mouth. I heard a woman bellow "Anesthesia," and, a minute later, someone tore me away from him.

"My, what a picture you look!" One of the emergency room nurses pulled me out of the ambulance. "We hear you had a real gang war down there at Lincoln!"

I nodded, still dazed. My mouth was coming out of numbness into bruised stinging. I touched my tongue to my lips, feeling their swollen strangeness. Angelo was being taken off by the trauma team.

"Here, you go get a cup of coffee, Bobby here will wait for you, won't you Bobby," she looked up at the driver. He nodded calmly, pulling on his pipe.

I went in, and the medical students assigned to Jacobi drifted around, trapped by my bloodied whites like small animals frozen in the headlights of an oncoming car. They made nonchalant conversation about trauma and gang war and other things we didn't understand. I barely heard them, the roaring darkness filling my ears as if I had crossed from another world and wasn't quite back into this one.

When I tried to go to the cafeteria, one of the aides stopped me. "You look disgusting with all that blood all over you. You can't go round people like that."

I looked at her. I needed a cup of coffee. I had no change of clothes with me. But in the well-lit hospital corridor, I knew I was inappropriate, wearing so much blood.

I went back out to the ambulance and climbed in the front.

The driver started the engine. "Got some coffee?"

"No," I said.

"Ah," he nodded, "people are like that."

We rode back quietly, smoothly. When we pulled up to Lincoln, he said, "I got another call. I'll just let you off." I slid off the seat and jumped to the ground.

"Thanks," I said. I looked up at his face, obscure in the dark of the cab. "Doesn't it bother you, ferrying people back and forth, night after night?"

He must not have heard me, because he didn't answer. Instead, the ambulance took off, swallowed again by the night, leaving me standing there alone.

The next morning I stopped by Jacobi on the way to Lincoln. There was no sign of "unknown male" on the neurosurgical ward or in the recovery room. I asked at the admitting office. They couldn't find him either. The clerk was busy, but she told me that usually, when they disappear like that, it means they died before they could get properly admitted.

When I got to Lincoln, the head nurse on days stopped me in the hall. She was an old friend of Marie's.

"So I hear you rode the ambulance last night." She was a large woman, and she looked down at me without smiling.

"Yes."

"Folks at Jacobi tell me you were giving that boy mouth-to-mouth when you got there. That's a good way to get all sorts of disease." She paused for a minute, as if she were going to say something more, then turned to go. "Remind me to teach you how to use the ambu-bag sometime."

Something of what I was feeling must have shown on my face, because she suddenly frowned and grabbed me by the shoulders. "Do you think you should have saved him? Who do you think you are? Better than you tried to save that boy's life, not just in one minute in the end, but year after year after year, and you some white girl gonna come down here and make everything all right in a few minutes?" She herself was shaking now. She pushed by me and ran down the hall.

I saw Marie later that night, as I came on the ward to order insulin for a diabetic. She was smoothing down the pillow for one of the chanters, the one with breast cancer. The old woman was out of her mind and didn't notice, but Marie was smoothing her pillow and pulling up her blanket anyway. I walked up to her.

"Anything else you need before I go to dinner?" I didn't look at her.

"I heard about you riding the ambulance with that boy that got shot."

"Yeah, well I didn't do much for him, did I?" I tried to turn away before she could say anything more, but she was too fast for me.

She fumbled in her pocket and pulled out some dog-eared Polaroids. "Here, let me show you something. My new grandbaby, just born last night. Isn't she beautiful?"

She smiled like the moon breaking loose on a cloudy night.

Sleep

The Stanton family, Therese, Stanley, and their daughter, Robbie, are home at six, just as the long slant of gravid sun splays across their polished floor. Spring sparrows toss through their window views, and, behind, a sapphire ocean lies vibrating jewels for their pleasure. Robbie Stanton is whining. She is a slight four year old, dark haired and wiry. She flips her body in the highchair like a fish on a line.

"If," shouts Therese, "you picked Robbie up earlier, she wouldn't be so crazed." Therese feels exhausted, sucked into a bog of fatigue. She is a poet; words clog and stopper, violent, inside her. The oven alarm buzzes, a pot of spaghetti erupts on the stove. I am dropping into a hole with no return, she thinks. Dog tired, crazy tired, bone tired. She has twenty different words for tired. She longs to go away, to the supermarket, to Algeria, anywhere quiet. Her specialty is philosophical poetry; she studies Plato, Aristotle, the Stoics, Epicurus. In imagining her life, she has not foreseen this quicksand of the minute.

"I had a late patient," says Stanley, taking off his blazer, sinking into the leather club chair, and putting his feet up on the ottoman. He looks down the knife-sharp crease of his pants to his Italian loafers, turning them first to one side, then the other. "Besides, she loves nursery school. Half the time, she doesn't want to come." He leans his head back against the chair and yawns, watching Therese and Robbie with a fond air.

"Turn that off," says Therese to Robbie, who has escaped the chair and turned on the television. "Come here and eat your dinner." Therese feels a swell of utter hatred toward Robbie. She takes a deep breath, closes her eyes, and smiles at her daughter. Robbie freezes, like a small nocturnal animal, suddenly illuminated. She runs back to the highchair. She stamps her foot, and her eyebrows contract. Her brows are dark and perfectly winged against her light skin. Her eyes are brown and yellow, her lips small, downturned and swollen, like a just-touched sea anemone. It is a carefully nuanced frown.

Therese sits in a dining room chair next to Robbie and puts her head on the table. She is tall, with striking long blond hair and pale eyes. She is six years older than Stanley and feels it. It makes her angry—and afraid.

"I've got a meeting tonight," says Stanley, leafing through the mail. There is an envelope from the county dental society. He rips the end and slides out the heavy, cream-colored paper.

"Did you," says Therese, cramming Robbie, who is squirming and struggling, back into the highchair, "send her to school with that stain in the middle of her blouse?"

Stanley reads the official notification of his induction as vice-president. "Hah," he exclaims with satisfaction. He looks at Therese. "We have to be there at seven." Stanley looks forward to these public occasions, where he is well liked for his easy-going charm and friendliness. He enjoys showing Therese off, stroking her hair and listening to her sharp wit in the presence of his colleagues. He feels she is somehow better than him, quick, and rare.

"I," says Therese, "am lecturing tonight. If I can stand up straight. I told you weeks ago." She scoops up some alphabet pasta with tomato sauce and shoves the spoon into Robbie's mouth. Robbie spits it out on Therese's dress and nylons.

Stanley says nothing. "Last night," he says after a minute, "was tough. Three A.M." He rubs his eyes. He reads the letter again and taps it against his thigh.

"If she doesn't start sleeping through the night," says Therese, wiping her clothes with a washcloth, "I'm going to die. Quite literally, die, expire, dust to dust. Or leave this house." She wants to slap Robbie, grab her arm, pummel her. She is falling asleep.

"You wouldn't leave," says Stanley, going to the kitchen and beginning to make himself a sandwich. "You'd miss her too much. Mother love."

"Yes," says Therese. "Mother love." She puts down the spoon. She sees, suddenly, Stanley's hygienist and the way the girl hangs on his every word. She feels the soft corrugation of her own forehead and the bitterness of her tongue. She imagines her colleagues standing on a cliff, analyzing the sea, describing, hypothesizing, clarifying, while she, Therese, feels the cold, the wet, the salt, she is *in* the sea, drowning. She gets up and leaves the room. Robbie begins to cry.

Stanley puts an apron over his suit and starts feeding Robbie. "Here, honey," he says gently. "Open your mouth." Robbie looks warily at him. He begins to make the spoon swoop and dive, and makes airplane noises. She smiles and opens her mouth like a bird-baby, waiting. He swoops the food into her mouth. She laughs, spewing alphabet pasta over the chair and the table. He laughs, too.

"We," he says to Robbie, "have to get you a babysitter." He dials the phone with one hand, while still feeding her with the other. He finds a babysitter, an older woman who arrives within a half-hour.

When Robbie finally finishes the pasta, Stanley yawns, eats his sandwich, cleans his hands, and sits to play the piano. Stanley was a music major, long haired and convinced of the importance of passion. Therese was a teacher of his; her gestures, her ironic comments, the toss of her hair, her published poems, her long slender legs, all of these contributed to his infatuation. She was flattered by this adulation. When he was not accepted into any conservatory, he decided to go to dental school instead. By then, they were lovers.

Stanley is playing Chopin with great affect and motion. He smiles. "This morning I realized," he calls to Therese, who is changing her clothes while giving instructions to the babysitter, "that I have everything I want in life."

Therese sighs and comes into the living room, buttoning her blouse. "I can't come to your dinner," she says. "It's the Thompson Prize Series; it's an honor I couldn't turn down." She is relieved he has stopped playing. She looks away. When she looks back, it is to deliberately admire his wide shoulders and the curl of hair that hangs down across his forehead.

"Robbie," Therese calls toward the bedroom, suddenly remembering this small formality, "what did you do in nursery school today?"

Stanley turns and looks at Therese. "You aren't coming?" he says. He stares at the living room wall. "But all the other wives will be there," he says. Therese can't hear Robbie's answer with Stanley talking, but she can tell it is short and angry. Therese sits next to Stanley on the piano bench. She feels too tired to get up and go in to Robbie, to ask her again. She leans her head against Stanley's shoulder.

"I'm afraid," she says, "I'm too tired to make sense tonight. I'm afraid I'll forget what I'm saying, just grind to a halt." She straightens her skirt. Stanley puts his arm around her, finally, with a little squeeze. Therese sags into him. She has excelled at every task placed in front of her, but the tasks keep coming, like little swells coalescing to a tidal wave. She sighs. She imagines herself walking on the revealed ocean floor, hands outspread, straight at the risen sea. Take me, she feels. Drown me.

"Don't go away," cries Robbie, who has darted into the living room, the babysitter hanging back, apologetically, in the doorway. "No Momma."

"Honey pie," says Stanley, "we'll give you a kiss when we get back." He smiles down at her and winks.

"No," says Robbie, who is lifted from the room, kicking, by the babysitter.

"Don't worry," says the babysitter, "she always stops the minute you drive away."

"No I don't," shouts Robbie from the bedroom, trying to bite the babysitter.

"Shush," says the babysitter to her. "Shush, sweetheart. We'll play little ponies as soon as they go." The woman puts Robbie down and straightens out her cotton print dress, rolling her eyes to herself.

She strokes Robbie's cheek. "Be quiet," she says, softly, "I'll give you candy, later." She picks up a picture book and waves it in front of the child, who momentarily quiets.

"Sometimes," says Therese to Stanley in the living room, "I worry I don't spend enough time with her." She smooths her nylons. She tries to feel control but wants only to go to sleep. *They* don't have to go through this, she thinks, of her colleagues, who are in the process of attempting to block her promotion to full professor. They have wives who shield them. So, she whispers to herself, does it make any difference to Robbie *why* her mother neglects her? As Therese thinks the word "neglect" her eyes fill with tears. She can't turn off her knife of a mind.

"Robbie's fine," says Stanley, thinking of how it will look, him being sworn in as vice-president, with no wife there. Therese has needs, too, he tells himself. "Really," he says, patting Therese, "I don't think kids need all this constant attention from their mothers. Makes them neurotic, if you ask me."

"Daddy," cries Robbie, dashing into the living room. She flings her arms around his legs. "Don't go. Please."

Stanley picks Robbie up, kissing her cheek, then throws her onto the couch. She giggles. He tickles her, bounces her on her head, flips her head over heels. "Got to go, sweet pea," he says. He holds her up to his face and lowers his voice. "Now, I don't want any of this waking up and coming into our room nonsense tonight." Robbie doesn't look at him. "I'm serious," says Stanley. "Big girls don't do that stuff."

"What about fathers," says Therese. "Don't children need their fathers?"

"Jesus," says Stanley. He yawns and shakes his head. "Relax." He feels fatigue seeping through him like a gradual ossification.

"Good-bye Robbie," says Therese, as she slips out the door. "I love you."

"Me too," says Stanley, and they each get in their cars and drive away.

That night, when Stanley returns, he tiptoes into Robbie's room and kisses her cheek. He feels substantial, the evening has gone well, with many compliments, and his hygienist there next to him, smiling and clapping. He estimates his income to be the second or third largest of the group. It is a well-earned dessert, after the hard years of training, making connections, setting up a practice. Robbie, in her radiant sleep, seems to him the most prized of his achievements, a satisfying end to an evening of confirmation. He strokes her small nose, brushes her ringlets back from her forehead.

Therese, completely enervated, skips washing, brushing her teeth, removing her make up, and falls, in her slip, into bed. She is distracted and consumed with comments and retorts, politics and promotions. She doesn't think of Robbie at all.

At two in the morning, Robbie stumbles into her parents' room, holding her blanket.

"Mommy," she calls from the doorway.

Stanley groans. "Go back to bed," he says.

"But I can't sleep," says Robbie, beginning to cry. "I need you."

"Go to bed," says Stanley, shouting.

"Mommy," says Robbie.

"Come on, sweetheart," says Therese, slowly trying to clear her reluctant mind. "You have to go back to sleep." It's happening again, she thinks. I am going to kill myself.

"Don't cater to her," says Stanley.

"You have any better suggestions?" says Therese, getting out of bed. "Come on," she says, staggering against the bedpost, "I'll make you some warm milk."

They sit in the kitchen while Robbie drinks the milk. Robbie watches her mother over the edge of the mug. "Mommy," she says, "I love you."

"You're going to have to go back to bed," says Therese. How am I going to teach in the morning, she thinks. How am I going to stand, walk, talk, breathe?

She holds Robbie's hand and leads her to the child's room. As they get to the threshold, Robbie pulls against Therese and starts to cry again. "Stop it," shouts Therese. "You are going to bed now, do you understand that?" She begins to twist Robbie's arm, then lets it go.

"No," wails Robbie. She cries with a particular loud, grating tone and flings herself down on the floor between the two rooms.

"Come on now," says Stanley, who has gotten out of bed and stands over her in his pajamas. "You have to go to your room."

"I want a book," says Robbie. "I can't sleep. I need a book." She cries for a few more minutes. Therese crawls back under the covers and curls up.

"Go get one," says Stanley, overcome with fury and yearning for sleep. "Hurry up. Just one." Robbie brings three.

After the books, Stanley picks Robbie up and puts her in her own bed. "No," she cries. "There are monsters." She clings to him. Bent over the bed with her hanging from his chest, he pulls one hand, then the other off his shoulders, but she has circled his waist with her legs. He lets go of her arms to pull off her legs, and she immediately grabs on to his pajamas, tight, with both hands. His back begins to hurt.

"Stop it," he shouts.

"No Daddy," she screams. "I'm scared." He finally pulls her off and drops her into the bed. She slips out of the bed and runs for the door.

"Robbie," says Stanley, sitting on her bed, holding his head. "Get back here." Robbie begins to cry, a loud, piercing wail.

"Just let her come in our bed," calls Therese. "I can't take it any more."

"Okay," says Stanley, sighing. "Mommie says you can sleep with us."

Holding her blanket and her doll, Robbie falls asleep immediately. She rolls against Therese, who lies, watching the illuminated dial on the clock read three, three-thirty, four. Stanley begins to snore. Therese pushes Robbie away, and the girl wakes slightly, opens her eyes, closes them, and flips, hard, against Stanley's stomach. He stops snoring. Robbie shifts again, hitting her head against Stanley's chest. He awakes.

"What time is it?" Stanley says.

"Five," says Therese, who sees the faint lightening of the curtains that presages dawn.

"Jesus," says Stanley.

In the morning, Stanley cannot get out of bed. He is thirty minutes late for his first patient. Therese struggles to dress Robbie, who will not stay still, will not wear what Therese picks out, and will not eat. When Therese drops Robbie at nursery school, Robbie begins to cry and cling. As she removes her, Therese feels that she is peeling off her own skin, flaying herself alive. In her office by nine, Therese is disintegrated, her brain is flying out of her head in spaghetti strands, like some psychotic Medusa. There is no possibility of writing. She locks the door, lies on the floor, and tries to sleep. Ten minutes later, her chairman knocks. "Therese," he calls, "Therese, are you in there?"

"It seems," says the child psychiatrist, a small fiftyish man with short hair and a blue blazer, "there is some role reversal here." He sits forward in the leather chair; his feet otherwise would not reach the floor. Stanley rubs his eyes and nods his head. He is dreaming of sleep.

"What," says Therese, "are you talking about." She is having difficulty controlling the world, which seems, in her fatigue, to be attacking her.

"It doesn't matter," says the psychiatrist quickly.

"We," says Therese, "*share* the childcare responsibilities." She wants to claw this little man. She looks sharply at the legs of his chair; they are writhing, wormy, and serpentine. She blinks several times, and reality holds.

"It's a small thing," says the psychiatrist, "sometimes we ask the child who she would go to if she were afraid, who reads her books at night, things like that."

Stanley wakes suddenly; he has fallen asleep for an instant, with his head still straight, as if he were awake. He hears the tone of Therese's voice. "Our marriage," he says, "is very happy. We love Robbie very much. Anything we can do to cure this little problem," he trails off expectantly.

"Yes," says the psychiatrist. "As I was saying, she is a bright girl, and very strong willed." He smiles carefully at Therese. "Perhaps, if you could find a way to spend more time with her?"

"Our pediatrician," says Stanley, raising his voice slightly, "thinks it may be a sleep disorder. Something organic." He puts his arm around Therese.

"I spend," says Therese, "a great deal more time with her than Stanley does. Whenever she's sick, whenever the nursery school decides to have a teacher day, whenever she needs to go to the doctor or the dentist."

"Yes," says the psychiatrist. "In any event, bright children find a way to get what they want, if you understand me?"

"No," says Therese, sighing. "I don't understand you."

"Perhaps," says the psychiatrist, crossing his legs, "the nursery school is strict. So the child decides to control what she can. Maybe the family's sleep."

Stanley moves closer on the couch to Therese. "What," he says, "are you telling us to do?"

"Perhaps give her a little more time, a little less structure during the day," says the psychiatrist. "Perhaps set a clearer limit at night."

"It doesn't matter what we do," says Therese, feeling herself beginning to tremble. "Nothing works. It's been years."

The psychiatrist considers her for a moment. "It is difficult," he says, "to be a parent. I don't mean to imply otherwise."

"What exactly," says Stanley, his voice rising slightly, "are you telling us to do?"

"Give her a day's warning," says the psychiatrist. "In the morning, tell her that if she wakes up that night, she cannot come in your room. Tell her again, before she goes to bed. Then, if she gets up, let her sleep in the hall or on her floor, but she cannot come in your room."

"She'll come in anyway," says Therese.

"It is important," says the psychiatrist, "to be very clear with children. You must be the one in control."

"She'll come in anyway," repeats Therese. Stanley nods and tightens his arm around her.

The psychiatrist pauses. "Not if you set an absolute rule," he says. "You are, after all, considerably bigger than her. And there are two of you."

The drive home takes over an hour; they have needed to find a therapist with no wife hidden in some department of the university and no staff appointment to a hospital where Stanley consults. Stanley drives, although Therese complains he will fall asleep at the wheel.

"I," says Stanley, "deal with fatigue better than you. You will brake for a hallucination. I'll keep the radio on."

It turns out, however, that they talk.

"I didn't like him," says Therese. "He seemed better when he was with Robbie."

"Yes," says Stanley, "but he's got a point. We have to take control. This is affecting my practice. I can't go to meetings at night, I can't go out to dinners any more." He rubs his eyes and yawns. His head feels unreasonably large, like a spongy balloon.

"I can't even think any more," says Therese. "Do you have any idea the pressure I'm under, the only woman with tenure, God forbid they should make me a full professor when I have a *child*. Lack of productivity. That's what they're going to say." Her voice rises. "Those *assholes*. As if any of them can write." How can I spend more time with Robbie, she thinks, when I'm fighting for my life. Why doesn't Stanley come home when she's sick? Why doesn't Stanley spend more time with her? Therese feels old, about to be divorced. I can't handle it, she thinks. She imagines single motherhood.

"Calm down," says Stanley, as Therese begins to cry. "We'll do what he says, we'll start tonight." Why do I have to deal with this when I'm trying to expand the practice, he thinks. Why doesn't she take care of it?

"But," says Therese, "we haven't seen Robbie since this morning when you took her to nursery school. And the sitter will have her asleep when we get back. What about warning her first?"

"This is a trained child psychologist," says Stanley. "We owe it to Robbie to follow his advice." He is concentrating on the road, trying to get home without an accident. He hates it when Therese cries; there are times he wishes she were a housewife and a little more appreciative of his success. "It's not good," he says, "for the child to have control over the parents. We must do what's best for her."

Therese pauses. "Yes," she says. She cries again for a minute, then wipes the tears on the back of her hand. "Yes," she says again. "I'm sure the psychiatrist is right."

Robbie is asleep when they get home. They pay the sitter. When they are alone, they embrace with sadness and resolution, undress, and fall into bed.

The first thing Therese hears, rousing from deep sleep, is a small, quivering voice. "Mommy," Robbie says. Therese is paralyzed, she cannot move. "I can't sleep," says Robbie, and there is a soft thud as she gets out of her bed. Therese feels an overpowering unwillingness to wake up. She struggles through dense fog.

Stanley rises up on one elbow and groans. "No," he shouts, "you stay in bed Robbie."

"I want warm milk," says Robbie, appearing at the threshold with her blanket.

"No," says Stanley. Robbie begins to cry. "No books either," he says. "You go back to bed."

"I can't sleep," wails Robbie, coming into the room.

"No," shouts Stanley, and he leaps out of bed. Robbie steps back; her eyes widen. She cries louder.

"These are the rules," says Stanley, standing over her. "You may not cross that bump into our room."

"Mommy," says Robbie, her voice rising.

Therese gets out of bed. She crouches in front of Robbie at the threshold. "No honey," she says, "you can't come in the room." Robbie shrieks and cries and stamps her feet. Therese stands up, next to Stanley, and they form a single barrier to the room. Stanley puts his arm around her.

"Go back to your room," he says, low and firm.

"There are monsters there," says Robbie. She tosses her short, tangled hair and tries to grab on to Therese.

Stanley pulls her off. "We," he says, "are going to bed now. You can go to your own bed, or you can stay in the hall, but you may not come past that bump into our room." He pulls Therese with him, and they get back into the bed.

"Mommy," says Robbie, "I love you." Therese gives a soft whimper and pulls the pillow over her head. She does not answer. Stanley reaches under the covers to hold her hand.

Robbie sees her parents draw away, and the darkness shifts and hardens. "Please," she calls. They do not answer. "Please," she screams. There is only silence, and the twisting of animals behind her. Her heart speeds, she begins to shake. "Daddy," she cries.

"If you keep crying," says Stanley, his voice clipped, "I will have to close the door."

"Daddy," Robbie screams.

"Oh God," says Therese softly.

Robbie cries on and on, a quarter, a half hour without letting up. Her hair is wet now with sweat. She is flushed from panic. Therese and Stanley lie in bed without moving. They think about the next day, they wonder how they will survive. Robbie screams higher and higher, uncontrolled. Therese cannot stand it, she feels that any moment she will scream, too. She hates Robbie, she wants to die. Stanley clenches and unclenches his hands. Finally, Therese makes a small guttural noise. Robbie cannot hear her, but she pauses, sensing something. She takes a step into the room.

"No," says Stanley.

"Stan," says Therese.

Stanley hears the desperation in Therese's voice and is filled with anger. He knows, suddenly, that this is a matter of life and death. He takes a deep breath, steels himself, and walks to the doorway. He lifts Robbie and moves her into the hall. He shuts the bedroom door in front of her.

It is quieter in their room now, Robbie's screams are muted, dulled and thickened, as if they belong to some other parents' child. Stanley lays his head against the pillow and sighs. After a moment, he clears his throat. "It's best for her," he says.

Therese spreads her arms and legs into the cool sheet on either side. She feels her body relaxing, longing, falling into dreams. She feels the possibility of giving in, of going, finally, to sleep. "Yes," she says.

Outside, Robbie does not stop screaming. She cries as long as she can before she gulps in air, then cries again. She cries until her nightgown is soaked with tears, her voice is hoarse, her heart pounds at an unbearable speed. Fear sweeps her shaking body, she hears shuffling, breathing, she feels the heat of eyes.

"Let me in," she begs, but she only croaks, her throat hurts and her voice doesn't come out right any more. She hits the door, again and again, they are coming at her.

"Mommy," she cries, "Daddy." She throws her small body against the door, lost. She drops on the floor, crying silently. She has fallen into a void of terror.

The next morning, the sun from Robbie's window deepens and glosses the fine hardwood floor of the hall. Robbie lies, a tangled curl, asleep outside the door of her parents' room. Her face is swollen, her hands are bruised.

"Hush," says Stanley, tiptoeing over her. The house is quiet and lovely.

"I actually," says Therese, "got some sleep." Stanley takes her hand and they walk to the kitchen. Therese looks at Stanley and feels fortunate, again, to have such a handsome husband. She leans against him as he fills the pot for coffee.

Stanley looks at her long hair and her elegant bones. He sees the space and glisten of the kitchen. He looks past the kitchen to the living room and the ocean beyond. He takes a deep breath. He squeezes Therese. "It was hard," he says, "but it was the right thing. For her."

"Yes," says Therese, leaning across him to flick on the coffee machine. "It is difficult to be a good parent."

These Days

But what could he do? What did he do?
What kind of a doctor was he, really?
—William Carlos Williams, *Old Doc Rivers*

       Hurry, Hi, lung crackles, breath whistle, death,
Trouble breathing? Beeper noise, hard table, green drape Look, I
didn't expect this to take so long (tucking a clean shirt into pressed
pants), I've got to go Press the bell lightly, always label the stetho-
scope with your name neatly printed on a piece of tape ambulance
siren, cardiac alarm How long have you felt this way? (a faint con-
cavity to his sturdy cheeks, he'll test positive) And this is what it's
come to, sediment of my years—impotent except to name the thing:

death. Not that I'm afraid, stared it in the face too long for that, but what do I teach the students?

When I was young, science was the rock of our foundations. I was my mother's only son, she wanted me to be a priest. A little biology, a little chemistry, I was so sure: in those days I liked to teach. Last week the chairman said to me, There're three sorts still in this business: the do-gooders, the disaster freaks, and the ambitious. Which am I?

Hey man, I'm telling you I don't shoot up nothing (tilting the chair back, looking at the ceiling) Well, maybe a few times, but I'm clean now, that stuff's bad for you, you know? (vein-scars down the arms.) Hair tufts, saber ribs, hurry, No, I haven't seen the 50 cc syringes. Some nodes are like gravel, these you don't worry about, some are like apricots long-forgotten under the seat of your car: hard with just a touch of rotten. These are of more concern.

In my day, when you were a houseman, you didn't get married, and you were damn happy if the hospital gave you hot meals, never mind a salary. Jimmy Arne went into the appendix business and raised four kids. Every Christmas he told me: Hey, there's a nice apartment opening up in our building, the wife worries about you, with just a room at work.

But it was a miracle to me, penicillin. We collected the urine after each dose, precipitated it out, and used it again. I never saw anything like it, little Lois Moran, two years old, stiffened up with fits from spinal meningitis, three shots and the fever left. I had my own microscope and centrifuge, how many students have I taught? Bless you Doctor, I think of you every day, Mrs. Moran wrote to me on a card edged with gold. I taped it on my wall.

Last week I got off on the fourteenth floor by mistake, I heard the machines and smelled the bitter solvents. Research labs there now: cold air through my skin; I stepped back into the elevator just as the doors were closing. Grants, papers, power, fame, and still they keep on dying. So young, they're all so young. Perhaps I should retire.

What Logos tells us: The genetic organization of the human immunodeficiency virus, cause of the acquired immune deficiency syndrome, is more complex than that of most known retroviruses. In dialysis arms of swirling serpent tubes, the yellow ooze of HIV-infected sera. On the blackboard, in the cool halls, the knife of the times: endonuclease, EcoR1. The purity of the DNA sample is usually the limiting factor in a successful digest; phenol, ethanol, EDTA, all can be contaminants. Concrete floors, green fluorescent light, and the buzzing of the autoclaves. Purify, cut, check, ligate, transform, sequence. Why does no one clean their bench?

I stayed here, I made this unit, no one believed Contagious Diseases could stand by itself. These are all my students now, every patient is my patient. What does it mean, *emeritus?* I have no other home. The hallways, the urinals, the narrow cots, these are my children.

It can get hot here, on the summer nights, the air doesn't move like outside. Was it our pride? The Book of Common Prayer says: fire and ice, winter and summer, winds. But, I ask, why do you call those you will not choose? I lie on the coarse white sheets waiting for sleep.

In 1944, Schatz, Bugie, and Waksman discovered streptomycin and stopped consumption in its tracks. I'm going in for medical, I told my mother. What good is a priest? And I laughed while she covered her ears. She died ten years ago, quietly, in her sleep, God be thanked. The halls of this hospital are green, they smell of iodine. At night in the emergency room, the cigarette butts coat the floor and smoke pierces your eyes like shards of ice. Why can't we stop it? They just keep coming smooth skinned: in his image created he them, why? To die?

I don't know what he did, You kids, get back here, I mean it, maybe he shot up, I don't think he ever went with men (hand over mouth), but I suppose you never know, I didn't ask, he was, you know (giggle) very private. (Bouncing the fretful baby) I was in love, you ever been in love? (Red and blue gigantic-flowered sundress, thin white sandals, red nail polish.)

Jimmy Arne's daughter was a nurse, nice girl. Last year she brought her baby by. Just for a minute, where the belly pushed out from the diaper, I ran my finger like a lizard across the warm, smooth skin. I never had a child, never really wanted one. The spirit is like the wind: you can feel it blowing, but you can't tell where it comes from. I grow older, and still I don't understand,

What the walls, floors, and bolted desks say: I am sterilization, vaccination, isolation, I am antibiotic, triumph. Tuberculosis, polio, smallpox, typhus, typhoid. Poultices, broths, rest cures, What a whining race, I spit clarity on a bisected path moving so that the sum of its distances from two foci is constant. I am Louis Pasteur with snake-necked flasks: the living forms that are found in liquids after fermentations do not spring up by themselves. I am Robert Koch with aniline dyes: to establish the specificity of a pathogenic microorganism, it must be present in all cases of the disease, inoculations of its pure cultures must produce the same disease in animals (when it is transmitted to such), and from these it must be again obtained and propagated in pure culture.

When this first started, I told the students: wait, you'll see. The lab boys'll take care of this. Mine was a lab with growing things, warm broth shaking in the bath, yeast and bacteria, the hot smell of bread and wine. That was in the old building, it's stone and rubble now, and in the endless meetings I nap, I dream: We're all busy, so I'll be brief. It seems there's been a problem with some workers refusing to draw blood on these patients. Some surgeons demand antibody testing. What will they do with the positives? Nurses who draw blood at the testing site want hazard pay. Housekeeping won't go in the rooms, garbage overflows, cafeteria won't bring the food. We must be very clear on our guidelines, on what exactly is expected.

You need an X-ray, CAT scan, gallium scan, MRI, bone scan, liver-spleen scan, upper-GI series, here, cough sputum into the cup, urine here, we need some blood, you'll need to see some specialists in consultation, bronchoscopy, endoscopy, maybe a lung, liver, skin biopsy. You're going to a single room on the third floor, don't forget to pay for the telephone and the TV, fill out this insurance form please, you should always bring your card with you, would you like to keep your valuables with you, or can someone take them home, you must take off your clothes and put on this gown, it flaps open that way on everyone, maybe I can find another one to wear over it, the other way around, don't forget the green foam slippers.

On the evening news, we all heard the cases of health-care workers. Health-care workers, how I hate these new names. What were they: doctors? nurses? In the endless meetings: the lab and the emergency room haven't stopped calling. What shall we do? The risk is very small. Some tend to get hysterical. It's probably best to gown and glove, what would you do, abandon these people? After work, I'll go to my room. I miss my lab. Was it a sin, these expectations we had of science? I'll go to my room, I've got a light and a good book.

From the regions of the liver, the spleen, and the tissues of the brain: We, lipid, protein, RNA, slither up the unsuspecting membrane, fuse, lipid/lipid, sliding slimy into that cell. We soil the cytoplasmic waters with our ribonucleotides: single-stranded, double-stranded DNA. And then we knife quickly, silently, into the core of the victim, who, never noticing, produces our proteins. They think that by naming us: RETROVIRUS, they will sap our power. Not yet.

I'm older now, my goals are thin. So many interns at City Hospital got tuberculosis, they had to make a night float system to give them some sleep, Johnny McGovern died anyway, and some young fellow the year before me too, I forget his name, tall young man, girlfriend was a nurse. They put him in that sanatorium, Meadow Lake. I myself turned positive on the skin test, my mother wrung her hands, she was standing in her streaked blue apron, and I laughed. Of course things were different then.

NO bum fucking, rimming, scat, fistfucking, biting, dildoes
NO bathhouses, bookstores, backroom bars

Them: Pink media swirls in sterile bottles, always work in the hood, gloves, gowns, Mozart on the radio, the oven has terminated its cycle early, this is where we grow, one ten-thousandth of a millimeter, Chinese boxes. Outer envelope of fat pierced by snakeproteins, inside that a covering, inside that the essence: ribonucleic acid. Cytosine, uracil, adenine, guanine. We float, coiled in perfect symmetry, we are far more ancient, what is the use of these pitiful namings, we call ourselves "I."

So, finally, I'll tell you what happened: I held a boy the other night, no more than eighteen, smart as a whip. He came in with pneumonia, middle of a sentence, just started coughing blood, fat black clots of blood. I saw his eyes widen and sweat bead up his cold face. There, I told him, there, it's all right. He was shaking so hard, he shook me with him. Page the lung man, I yelled at the nurse, but the blood wouldn't stop coming. Now he was vomiting scarlet, and it rained down soft and warm on my arms, he was staring at me, pleading, trying to talk words that blossomed into blood. Page him, I shouted, as I felt the boy slip through my arms. Saline, IV, Blood, Call a Code, hurry. I pushed my palms down into his chest and felt the crunch of ribs. Now there were others helping me, the needle pierced wax skin, tubes, machines. Push, pull, fluid, air, yelling, pumping, young doctors get very good at this. His body jerked with each push, and I looked at his face, at his blank eyes, oh God have mercy, he was just a child. Dead and we pound on and on. . . . Plump cheeks his mother cleaned each morning, soft hair his father stroked goodnight. *Stop* I said. They pulled away, looking at me in confusion, the nurses and interns and residents and students. But they pulled away. I am an old man. And I knelt on that pocked linoleum floor: forasmuch as it hath pleased Almighty God . . . *pleased.* I cannot comprehend such pleasure.

So, in the end, I have drained, become hollow, neither doctor nor priest. Too much data, AZT, protocols, viral coats, and still they die without pause, relentless. Touch, heal, cure, it's past now, and I'm past too, like the leaves that rustle down city streets.

A friend of mine goes to all the wakes, funerals, shiva-sittings, rites, requiems, memorial services, interments, burials, entombments. He keeps his black suit hanging in the office so he can go straight, white coat, black suit, white coat. I, myself, stand at my window looking at the trees sticking up like hairbrushes in the ruptured street. Forgive me, but I have loved this work. The wind comes now, I feel it touch against my cheek.

Shambalileh

On the morning after her fourth miscarriage, Shadee sank, weighted by Oreos and grief, into the pristine velour of the rear seat of her minivan. Where she had waited for ground-in animal crackers, there was only the faint impression of an occasional newspaper or briefcase. Where she had tinted the glass to shield a sleeping baby, there was only the impenetrable privacy through which she peered. Get it darkened, the other secretaries where she worked at the time had told her. It gets hot. Besides, whispered a young mother when they were alone together at the copying machine, I don't like the idea of all those strangers eyeing my kid, you know what I mean?

And so, five years later, Shadee sat with the doors locked, curled into the back where no one could see, and considered the stripped trees of November, their scarlets and yellows mashed into a sullen brown by the incessant rain. It had been raining since Joe left. Screw him, she thought, and ate another Oreo. Joe was a chemist at Brown. He was giving a paper on ionophores in Santa Barbara.

Shadee looked through the woods at the glittering sliver of Olney Pond. Like an ice pick, she thought, and thought of Munch, and dismissed the thought. The verticals of the bare trunks composed themselves into the only picture she had of her brother: standing, back to a peeling but ornate wood pillar that barely supported a patterned ceiling over the porch of her grandfather's mansion in Shiraz. Your father's family was wealthy, her mother told her, and, growing up in the skittering ratholes of New York, she drank in this knowledge mixed with the musty spice sauce that always covered the rice and meat. But now, she looked at the photograph and saw only a small boy in a checked shirt and baggy pants, standing by cracked steps, in front of rows of potted geraniums and a sagging porch. They kept my baby, her mother said, and wept. Shadee never said: aren't I your baby, too? They let me take the girl but kept the boy, her mother would tell each new acquaintance. That's me, Shadee told herself. The girl.

Shadee was unsure if she, herself, really wanted children. In the beginning, it had been Joe who bought the house backed up to Lincoln Woods, so he could take the children fishing, and bought the van, to be prepared. All those years of pills and IUDs. What a joke. You married me to get a green card, Joe teased her. It was true they'd been illegal, overstayed a visitor's visa, her mother and herself. But she married Joe because he would be a good father. And now, their children had presented themselves in flight, slipping the world in a stream of clotted blood. Shadee pulled her eyes away from the barren woods and picked up the newspaper. She turned the pages until she came to Unfurnished Apartments, one room.

A mansion, her mother had said, over and over. And it was dreaming the decayed mansions of childhood and Persia, and the black-and-white ghost of her small brother, that she blamed for never finishing her degree in art history, never staying in a job past one promotion, never planning, never advancing, never, as her friends put it, fulfilling her potential. The ovulation timings turned to the smell of geranium leaves pressed into hot dust, the hormone treatments to the feel of the pumice stone on her elbows and feet, the artificial insemination to the fragrant hours of the bath. She remembered women talking on intricate carpets, the leisurely preparation of a meal. And after the *in vitro*, which cost all their savings, the musty smell of spice, the spice that meant Iran, the spice that wore its way into everything: sheets, walls, her mother's hair. The pungent smell of loss.

How can you not know the name of that spice? Joe had asked her once, incredulous, as she unwrapped a jelly jar filled with its dried green leaves, sent from her uncle in Los Angeles. Joe always remembered things, thought Shadee. Perhaps that was why she married him, so that he would annotate her life.

"Quiet room, separate entrance." She pulled a pen from her purse and marked the ad. She would be late from her lunch break. She would dye her hair red, go back to school, and she wouldn't care about anything.

Why can't we adopt? said Joe. A Korean, a Romanian, hell, what's wrong with this little girl here? And he would show her a picture in the paper of a little girl with *spina bifida* wearing a leg brace. Advertising children like puppies from the ASPA, Shadee thought, and felt sick at the photographs, at herself. Why not? he asked, rubbing her back. And she would look away from him, her tongue tied into the peppermint scent of geraniums reflected in the mirrors hung along her grandfather's porch.

When Joe got back from the airport, Shadee made scrambled eggs and served them to him, reaching over to pour his coffee and lighten it with milk. She had arranged a bowl of fruit in the center of the table like a slightly messy still life. Cezanne, she thought. For the asymmetry of their relationship. She had forgotten how the hair curled down the back of his neck, and she had a sudden urge to ask him, again, why did you marry me? But he always said the same thing: because you're interesting, because I'm boring. It left her slightly unsatisfied, as if there was more, something between the ions and the term papers, the television football games and going fishing, that he wasn't explaining.

When he finished his meal, she sat down, staring at him across the green vinyl table. "I'm leaving you," she said, when he looked up, questioning.

"Ah," he said, then hesitated. "We lost the baby?" She could see the sorrow rearranging his face and hated him for it. She ran to the bathroom, locked the door, and sat on the toilet.

"Shadee," called Joe, tapping on the bathroom door. To Shadee, his voice carried the weight and domesticity of his parents in Redwood City. Joe's father was assistant game warden for Alameda County; his mother, a secretary. Joe had visited them on his way home. That was another reason she'd married him. Because his parents wore nylon and polyester, because they'd welcomed her with open arms. She enjoyed hating him for this. Her own itinerant mother wore only natural fibers and was on her fourth unhappy marriage.

"I'm leaving you," she shouted to Joe, through the door.

"Let's go for a walk," said Joe, pressing his face to the doorjamb. There was a long silence. "Come on, honey," he said. Shadee opened the door and pushed by him to sit on the couch, her face streaked with tears. "I'm sorry," he said, "that I was gone."

"I wouldn't," said Shadee, "want to interfere with your career."

"Shadee," said Joe carefully, pulling out his fishing poles from the closet. "I asked if you wanted to come to Santa Barbara with me."

"Say it in Persian."

"Shall we take the van? Or walk?" Joe put on his jacket and unhooked Shadee's from the coat rack. Before they left, he excused himself for a minute, walked down the hall to the back bedroom, shut the door, walked across the room and pounded the far wall with his fist. When he felt the pain of the bruised knuckle, he returned.

"Mom and Dad say hello," said Joe, swinging the van around Grandview Avenue and into Lincoln Woods. Shadee didn't tell him she'd been to the woods herself the day before, or that she was about to be fired for missing two days in a row.

"I don't want children," she said, staring straight ahead, down the road.

"Okay," said Joe. "Jesus, those colors, I really missed that in California, the fall leaves."

"What do you mean, 'okay,'" she shouted.

"Look," said Joe, pointing at a brown rabbit that lurched across the road and into the underbrush. "Do you want to invite your mother to visit?" He pulled the van into an empty picnic site near the pond.

"I hate you," said Shadee.

"Deer tracks," said Joe, sliding from the van and pointing to the damp, black ground.

"Screw you," said Shadee, and she went to sit on a rock overlooking the water. Joe sat down next to her and sighed. Shadee watched his unshaven chin, where the stubble was beginning to show, but he didn't speak. She turned and looked through the clear water of the pond to the silvery flickers below. She remembered the goldfish she'd had as a child. Fat fringes waving in their small pool, even her brother had acknowledged they were hers. Joe impaled a nightcrawler and cast. The line floated through the air and dropped noiselessly to the bottom, where it transformed the glassed surface into endless concentric circles. Joe propped his rod in a forked stick. And then they sat, looking out at the pond and the cold blue day.

"There was a guy at the meetings," said Joe, "from UC Berkeley, with a way of layering membranes I think we can use. If that new postdoc ever does any work." Shadee didn't answer. Joe glanced at her face, but she was staring out at the line, where it disappeared into the water. He waited, but she still did not move. He remembered the first time he had seen her, in college, how frighteningly fierce she had seemed, how beautiful. It was still there, he thought, underneath.

"I always thought," he said, finally, to her stony profile, "we would have children." Shadee felt the images knife through her: Joe playing with friends' children, Joe teaching the neighborhood kids to fish, her brother running through the streets of Shiraz crying, Shadee, Shadee, turn the spigot, and suddenly a flood of water rushed down the open gutters and into the waiting houses where the women and children opened the basement cisterns. She remembered particularly the high call of his voice.

"My apartment is on College Hill," she said. "I put down a deposit." She was still watching the line when, without warning, a fish leapt from the hidden depth below. Suddenly the water began to ripple and Joe grabbed the fishing rod. She got up and turned away, not wanting to see the creature yanked from his waters, gasping and twisting.

"You're feeling sorry for yourself," said Joe, and she turned to see him holding the fish against the flat surface of the rock. It was a stocked rainbow, its delicate pink and yellow-green gleaming in the late morning sun. Jean Baptiste Simeon Chardin, thought Shadee. French realism.

"You wouldn't understand," she said. Joe turned and stared at her. He's angry, she thought with surprise.

"We're all lonely, Shadee," he said. "When I was *five* I knew I was different from my parents and always would be."

"They love you," said Shadee.

"Yes," said Joe, reaching into his bag. "As best they can. Just like I choose to love you, as best I can."

Shadee felt rage and longing wash up through her. She looked down at her own trembling hands. "There is a certain arrogance that comes," she said, "from having always had what you needed, at the time you needed it."

"Seems to me," said Joe, "there is a certain pleasure in always seeing oneself as a victim." He unsheathed a long, thin-bladed knife. I should turn away, thought Shadee, but the grace of his thick fingers lightly touching the gasping fish, the power of the tableau, held her. Suddenly Joe made a single, downward cut, just behind the gill cover, to the backbone. The trout gave one last twist. Joe slit deeply along the backbone right down to the rib cage, nearly to the tail. He sliced easily, swiftly, the flesh from the rib cage, flipped the fish over, and repeated it, revealing the abdominal contents, which spilled against the grey rock: stomach, intestines, liver, kidneys, heart. Joe cut off the head, then swept the head and entrails off the rock into the pond, where they sank with hardly a ripple. Shadee felt herself begin to shake. She ran behind the van, where Joe couldn't see her, and vomited up the toast and eggs she'd had for breakfast. When she was done, she wiped her mouth on her sleeve and walked back to the rock. Joe had packed away the fillets, leaving only a small damp spot where the fish had been. He was sitting with his legs pulled up in front of him, looking at her. He belongs to that rock, she thought, that water, these woods. She saw his eyes on her hair, her black Persian hair, her brown skin, and felt the pull of him as involuntarily as the fish, flickering below, mouthed their way toward prey.

"Shadee," said Joe, and she heard him as if underwater. "Shall we go home?" Ten years of marriage, she thought. How innocent one is at twenty-one, how much you think you can understand.

As Joe turned the van onto their street, Shadee finally spoke. "I'm not going to live with these fucking lawns and their fucking tricycles any more." Joe didn't answer. "I'm going back to school. I'm going to trade in the van for something small."

Joe pulled into their driveway and turned off the ignition. "Okay," he said, looking away from her, out the window. "I always thought you should finish your degree. Get a job in a museum or something."

"So we could *both* rush around obsessed by work," said Shadee.

"Do you think this is what I wanted?" shouted Joe suddenly. "Nobody asked me: do you want your wife to have four miscarriages, go crazy, and start to hate you?"

Shadee looked at him, how he clenched his hands around the steering wheel, how his ears had turned red under the blond hair. *"You're feeling sorry for yourself,"* she said. "You want to say you hate me."

Joe sank his head onto the steering wheel. "It doesn't matter," he said.

Shadee sat very still, watching him as if he were a new species, something she had never encountered before. "I love you," she said. Joe reached out and pulled her next to him. She began to sob. "Each time," she whispered, after a moment, "I imagine."

"Hush," said Joe, holding her, and they sat together, in the driveway of their ranch house, weeping.

The next day, Shadee pulled out the Rhode Island College bulletin she had stuck under the phone book in the hall. As she looked at the listings, computer science, electrical engineering, music history, she began to dream of Iran, of return, of her brother. She felt her mouth twist into Persian, and memory, and she knew it was a way of blaming Joe. She tried to be fair, to force herself into the truth, but the feeling was too great. She wanted to belong somewhere, to someone, even in hate.

Joe came home late that night, after a day spent in the silence of the lab; calculate, set-up, pipette, vortex, centrifuge, decant, measure, record. He found Shadee asleep. He looked carefully at her still face, as if trying to decipher her language, her expectations. He touched her cheek with his bruised finger and found that he was trembling.

"Shadee," he shook her awake.

"Yes," Shadee said, smoothing the hair over his red ears. She got out of bed and put water in the machine for coffee. Joe sat down and watched her. "Joe," she said finally.

"Yes," said Joe, feeling himself begin to sweat.

"I called my uncle," she said. "I asked about my brother."

"Shadee," said Joe. "Please."

"My brother," said Shadee, "won't talk to me. Not even after all these years. Afraid I might pollute his wife and daughter."

"You aren't really moving out, are you?"

"You wouldn't understand," said Shadee. "My little brother."

Joe put his head down on the table. "I don't understand. Is that what you want me to say?"

"Yes," shouted Shadee.

After a moment, Joe got up and started pouring the coffee. "Okay," he said. "I don't understand." He went to the refrigerator and got the milk. "Is there anything else you would like me to say?"

Shadee looked at his pale face, at the darkness under his eyes, the swelling of his eyelids. She began to laugh. "Who the fuck understands anything?" she said, walking over to the cabinet and taking out the bag of Oreos.

"Please stay," said Joe. "Please, Shadee."

Shadee looked at him a long time. She watched the back of his neck as he bent over his coffee. She thought about the years in college and after college, the miscarriages. She thought about her parents, and his. She looked out the window and saw Joe and herself reflected, shimmering, like fish in the dense pool of night. She got up and walked around to Joe. "I've been thinking," she said, resting her hand on his shoulder, "about adoption."

"Yes," he said.

Shadee sat back down in her chair. "My uncle," she said, after a while, "told me the name of that spice. 'Shambalileh.'" She spelled out each letter.

"Good," said Joe, seizing a pen and holding it, knifelike, in his familiar fingers as he wrote down the word. Shadee turned away and stared out the window.

"It's okay," said Joe, after she'd been quiet several minutes. "Everything will be okay."

Shadee watched the images of herself and Joe, disembodied, floating and interpolating in the shadows of the white colonial across the street. Chagall, she thought. Underneath their arms and faces, she saw the thick form of the minivan, sunk solidly, like a submerged rock, in front of their house. She laughed and took another Oreo. "Sure," she said to Joe, "no problem." And, with great caution, she began to imagine the rest of her life.

Sightings

       They found him slung across a limb down by the frozen pond, like some careless boy's shirt. Philip imagined that when he stiffened into bloody ice, the panther felt only surprise. Astonishment, maybe, at the musket blast that dropped him from the tree, the knifing, the endless bludgeoning, and then the stone that crushed his skull with such ambition that one eye popped from the socket, slid like a boiled egg across the crusted snow and came to rest aimed up at the opaque November sky. To Philip, these episodes presented themselves as tableaux: the hunt, the death, the people, their cornfields and pastures tattooed on the hillsides, spread across the panthers' land. Stills of a violation, a failure of some catamount rule of grace.

It was another child's grandfather who first told Phil the story—the Ledbergs had come to Vermont each summer since the thirties, when Gloria, Philip's mother, inherited the cobbled farm of her father's cousin, whose death brought to an end that branch of the family's stony subsistence. Philip's mother wanted to sell, but Bernie, his father, scrubbed the farmhouse floors, bought plywood furniture with gaudy print fabric, hung oils of big-eyed children on the walls, and hooked up a phonograph to the generator so he could play Tommy Dorsey while he looked out at the stars. When his mother finally conceived, she quit her job teaching school but started again a year later to pay the bills. Each vacation, Philip played up and down the dirt road with the Smith children while his father drove dreamy miles across New England trying to sell cake decorations, instant topping mix, always something new. Philip wasn't to tell the Smiths, who farmed at the bottom of the hill, that his mother worked back in New York, or that his gentle father, who visited on summer weekends, was unable to support them.

His mother was dead now, but he could still smell the faint air of accusation that stilled the gingham curtains and perfumed the folded sheets. His father, hunched apologetically alone into old age, sat on the porch with Mr. Smith drinking seltzer and looking out across the open meadows to Hogback Mountain.

"Don't believe it's panther they're seeing," said Mr. Smith, setting the newspaper on the table next to his beer. "No prints." He'd come up the road to get away from his daughter, who had brought with her his youngest grandchild, sick and irritable with a cold.

"But look at the deer," said Philip's father, "spilling over everywhere, just waiting for them. It makes sense, by God, I believe it." He glanced over at Philip, who was looking into the distance, not listening to the conversation. The word "deer" had made him think of his daughters, especially when they were younger, with less polish of civilization over their fierce tangled hair and curiosity. Suddenly and painfully, he missed them. He'd come out from California, left the entire issue of his failure in medicine, to help pack his mother's clothes, to sort things, air out the place. To put aside his own problems and let his father talk about his grief. He'd come expecting to find his father, who'd been so dependent, overwhelmed by this first summer without his mother. Instead, he found him obsessed with animal ecology.

"Maybe zoo runaways, but not breeding females," said Mr. Smith, scratching his head. "There'd be tracks. You think them panthers just float through the forest?"

"I'll get some chips," said Philip. "Anyone want a refill from the kitchen?" He moved toward the door.

"Remember Wardsboro?" said his father. "If they couldn't tell bear from panther those days, what makes you think they can now?" He offset the aggressiveness of the question with a small smile and drummed his fingers on the table.

Mr. Smith shifted his angular body in the rocking chair. "You should hay that south meadow. The woods'll take it back, faster than you imagine." He rocked a few more minutes, then added, "Never did believe that old catamount story. Before I was born, you know."

"It was light snow," said Philip suddenly. "And there were tracks. They were sure it was a bear." He looked at the tortuous veins of his father's hand rising under the skin as thin as a fetus's and thought of his own fiftieth birthday coming up. And of his chairman's statement that he should leave—and who could blame the man after Philip lost his grants and lab? Philip closed his eyes. He had a peculiar gliding sensation, an image of himself obscenely boyish for his age, drifting a few inches off the ground, between his medical-school classmates, who had thickened and rooted over the years. I am a doctor, he told himself. But he didn't believe it. He had always been a painter. First a young and promising painter, then a failed painter. Even when he hadn't held a brush or smelled oils in twenty-five years.

"You okay?" said his father.

"Sure," said Phil, and he went out to the kitchen. He pulled a bowl from his mother's well-organized closet. Reaching for the chips, he brushed a glass off the counter and it splintered on the floor. Shards caught in the uneven floorboards, composing themselves into line and texture of image. Phil ignored it and swept up. He could hear them on the porch, still talking about the Wardsboro panther.

They had come asking for a rifle, the way Philip remembered imagining it, and so the man had gone with them, pulled along, without really thinking it out. A young bear, they said, and they tracked him in and out of the narrow strips of woods, past depressions in the dried leaves where he'd lain, past where he'd downed a small doe and slit her open with one quick swipe, past an old windfall where he'd rested a moment after his meal, until it got too dark to follow. The panther had no idea they were on his tail, he was so intent on his own hunting and so innocent of the experience of prey.

Afterwards, the man never knew what made him look up to see the great cat lying there, one sleek paw combing the bitter air. Nor did he know that he'd fired the musket until the catamount fell and started to run, crashing lopsided with his broken shoulder through the underbrush. All the man remembered was the yellow eyes, staring at him with their gravid pupils, and the extraordinary stillness of the moment, like the instant before the grunt of birth. Then the panther snarled, and the man realized it wasn't that he'd thought the tracks were bear. He'd known they were.

Floating, thought Philip, and he imagined a panther gliding between pines, while below a sinuous trail of ghost bear prints formed in the snow. He looked around the kitchen, poured some potato chips into the bowl, and brought them out to the porch. A light wind had picked up across the valley. The Vermont forest lay as it always had, in his memory, in his imagination, beautiful, leafed and unleafed, a subtle gathering of hope. Philip felt the breeze cool his cheeks and lift through his hair as it slammed the kitchen door.

———————————

Once, Philip had watched Mr. Smith skin a rabbit he shot in the upper meadow: one swift slit, then soft fur and fat peeled off like a wet bathing suit, leaving the fascia and tendons, the bulging abdominal sac exposed. That was how Philip looked at the land now, scalping the maples and evergreeens, the black-eyed Susans, the bluebells, the day lilies in all their voluptuous color, the long blond grasses, the black topsoil off the surface of the land until there was only stone. It was structure revealed, like gross anatomy, like Philip's life, he thought.

The naming, the firmness of success, all camouflage. And it was stripped from him now. He was pounding down the dusty path from Stratton Mountain to the West Wardsboro–Arlington road. It was clear his father didn't need him—before Philip got up that morning his father had his mother's clothes mostly packed. Philip remembered his pride, in grade school, when his friends all wanted to play at his house, because his father was there, because he was nice. And his shame, later, when asked what his father *did*. Philip had hated his father for this weakness, this not being successful.

"Look at this, Phil," his father said, raising his voice from the living room, where he was reading the newspaper. "Another one. Over in Jamaica, spotted by a tree cutter. Drinking from the shallows of a pond." He shook the paper at Philip. "That's close," he said. "I bet if you keep your eyes open," he was watching Phil and didn't finish the sentence.

Philip rubbed his eyes. There were stacks of wildlife books spread across the coffee table that his mother had kept so clean. And there was a dried mud print on the high gloss where his father had propped his boot.

His father caught the glance. "You know I told Mary there was no need for you to come out here," he said, looking guilty, "and leave your work." He reached his hand toward Philip with a gesture of deference.

"That's okay," said Philip, "I wanted to come." It was then that he decided to spend the day hiking.

When he came back down the Long Trail to where his car was parked, it was already late afternoon. Even so, he found himself turning off the road back to South Wardsboro and bumping along graded gravel to the Wardsboro pond he'd gone swimming in as a boy. Sometimes he'd gone with the Smiths, but sometimes his father brought him, and the two of them roughhoused in the water, carefree. He thought of his own daughters and how he had played with them at that age, what was it, eight? Ten? It was too cool now to swim, and besides, the land was clearly private. He smiled to himself. The land was probably private then, too, but a boy doesn't notice those things. He stopped the car in a cloud of dust and got out.

Across the pond sunlight knifed through the still, red maple leaves and dappled the glassy water. Phil sat on a log swatting deerflies for a while, then he stood up, squinting into the overhanging branches, watching, waiting. I should get back, he thought. But he pictured his father, reading the newspapers, listening to the radio, and grew suddenly restless. Failure, he thought, and the word sank into the marshy shallows, permeating the humid air. He could barely approach the thought of losing his job, of money—the mortgage, the lessons, the food bill, college for the girls. "Look at it as an opportunity to go into private practice," Mary, his wife, had said. "You're lucky, a doctor can always retrain."

Philip began to tramp the edge of the pond, crackling and crashing through the dense underbrush. He remembered the feeling of the day he'd gone into the premed office at college and signed up. "What's an art major like you doing here?" the advisor had asked.

"Don't you think I can do it?" Phil had asked defensively. He wanted to be premed forever.

Phil's eyes searched trees, thickets, hiding places between the pines. He paused in a clearing, listening. Maybe here, in sight of his childhood, he would understand what to do next. Nothing moved in the forest, except the drone and dive of insects. Phil sighed. As he turned to leave, he saw that he was surrounded by a chancel of dust, hot and radiant.

The next evening Phil sat beside his father reading, uneasily, a dusty thirty-year-old paperback mystery he'd found on the bookshelf in the bedroom.

"Phil," his father said suddenly, his voice strained.

Phil saw his father's pale face and the hand against his chest. "Here, swing around and lie down," he said. He picked up his father's feet and carried them in an arc, onto the flowered fabric of the couch. "What's the matter?" Phil felt himself constrict.

"It's nothing," said his father firmly. "Put me back." He tried to sit up and fell back again, with a groan. Phil thought his lips were turning slightly blue.

"I'm calling the fire department," said Phil. He began to walk across the room, feeling his heart pound. I should be able to handle this, he thought. A doctor should be able to handle this.

"Take them an hour to get up here and back out to Brattleboro," his father said, tightly now. "Better take me in the Ford." He sat up and hunched over, running his fist up and down the center of his chest.

Oh my God, thought Phil. It's real. He's having a heart attack. He ran outside and pulled the car up to the front door. "Here," he said to his dad, "let me carry you."

"It's just a little indigestion," said his father, but he went with Phil, leaning on his arm.

"How long has this been going on?" said Phil, when his father was settled in the car and they were on their way down the long dirt road into Newfane.

"It's nothing," said his father, looking out the window. "Anyway, it's stopped."

Phil let out his breath. Angina, he thought. Crescendo angina, he could infarct any minute. He pressed his foot against the gas, raising a cloud of dust behind them.

The emergency room was cold and painfully bright. When a nurse put her arm around his chest and held him up, he realized he was shaking. When she offered him coffee, he found he couldn't straighten his fingers to take it, so she left the cup next to him on a chair. He stared at the cubicle wall, smelling that bitter emergency-room smell, the one he associated with his career, with medicine: disinfectants, panic, pressure. He sat, motionless, the entire hour it took the nurses to speak to his father, run a cardiogram, and wait for the doctor to examine him.

"I think," said his father from the gurney, after the nurses left, "it's stress."

"Maybe it's losing mom," said Phil.

His father didn't answer, so Phil turned to look at him. A tear had run down his father's face, and he was wiping it with the thin blue-and-white robe they'd dressed him in. "Not really," his father said. After a moment, he added, "I think I miss working."

"Working," said Phil.

"I really enjoyed my job," his father said. "I was so fortunate to have work I liked."

Phil stared at his father with sudden anger. He couldn't think of what to say. He remembered how, in college, he would say, "My father's in business," knowing the other boys' fathers were lawyers, architects, doctors. And later, he would tell his special girlfriends, when they remarked on his father's warmth and generosity, about the difficulty of trying to become a man with no model of success.

"Mary," he said, loudly, "can't support the family, and I wouldn't expect her to." He felt immediate remorse. Why was he badgering his father at a time like this?

His father turned to look Phil in the eye. "You always were," he said, "such a determined boy."

"Mary," Phil said later, calling from the pay phone down the hall, after she accepted the charges.

"What's wrong?" said Mary.

"Nothing really," he said. "Dad had some chest pain. It might be angina, but they think it's probably just indigestion. They'll do a stress test tomorrow."

"He's okay?"

"Sure," said Phil. "Now we can go back to panthers." He cleared his throat. "Maybe," he said, "Dad and I will drive around a little, take a look at New England. You know how he loves to drive and see the scenery, like he used to, when he was working."

"Phil," said Mary, after a pause, "the department called, they want your lab and your office packed up and cleared out by the beginning of classes."

"I *hate* medicine," said Phil.

"You'll be happier," said Mary, "out of academics, on your own."

"I don't think I can do it anymore," said Phil.

"Phil," said Mary, her voice rising, "we have children, we have financial responsibilities, you know."

"Maybe," said Phil, "you can go back to nursing."

For a minute, Mary didn't say anything. "It's been so long," she said, finally, and her voice cracked. "It doesn't make sense. What about the children, after school?"

"I don't know," said Phil.

"You can make as much money in a day, as a doctor," said Mary, "as I could ever make in a week."

"Yes," said Phil. "Of course, you're right."

Fifty, he thought, as he waited in front of the hospital for his father. Dawn was beginning to lighten the thin eggshell of clouds into pink translucence, clarifying the stand of pines across the hospital lawn. Phil found himself imagining how he would mix the colors, the feel of the canvas, the brush. The smell of the oils. Stop it, he told himself. Just as he turned away, something stirred against the shadows. When he turned and looked again, it had disappeared.

"Dad," he said, opening the car door for his father. "Let's drive around some tomorrow. I've got to go back soon." He touched his father's arm. "I lost my grants," he said. "They fired me."

His father nodded and watched the road ahead. After a while he said, "Your mother never understood why I liked driving so much."

"No," said Philip, "she didn't."

"I like," said his father, "a little time to think. A little peace and quiet. Freedom."

"Don't make much that way," said Phil.

"No," said his father. "It wasn't what your mother expected." After that, they drove in silence.

"Hey," said his father suddenly, pointing into a grove of trees beside the road. Philip didn't answer. He stopped the car and sprang out, running up towards the woods, then stood, searching the trees. "Phil," said his father, who had labored up the hill after him. He stood over a muddy patch in the dried grass. In the center was a paw print, three or four inches across.

"How delicate," said Philip. "As if the animal weighed nothing at all." He glanced around into the silence. "Whatever it was, it's gone now," he said. "Let's go home." He started back to the car.

"Wait for me," said his father.

So Phil stood, just inside the grove, as his father returned slowly and carefully across the twigs and stumps. Pines warmed and released their fragrance, squirrels skittered to and fro, beetles crawled over his shoes. Phil took a deep breath of woods and felt something stir in himself, as if the sky expanded, as if time slowed until there was enough. He stilled, and watched, and waited. He felt afraid.

"You see," said his father, when he reached Phil, "how they made that mistake, the similarity to bear."

Philip stood for a minute without answering. "No," he said finally. And in that moment he knew he had chosen, and that he would cause his wife and children pain. "No," he repeated, looking at his father. "With bear you see the claws." And then he helped his father, carefully, back into the car.

Juilliard

For Tammy

Lynette was dead.

"How sad. Such a talent," said Anna Mikolich, who had, briefly, been her roommate. She crossed her legs carefully, displaying the slender calves.

"Oh my God," said Michael Rubin. He glanced at his hands, which were shaking from shock and a small amount of cocaine. The finals of the Leventritt would be in September. He had never won a competition in which Lynette was also entered. "No," he said. "Not Lynette."

"Yes," said Anna, a bit curt this time.

"Oh, Jesus, how?"

Anna sighed. She leaned over and whispered in his ear. "Pregnant. She was pregnant."

"But I just saw her last week," he said, beginning to cry, "at that bar, the one near Columbia." He lifted his head suddenly and looked at Anna. "Has anyone," he asked, "told Heinrich?"

They were sitting backstage at the Vermont Music Festival, on overstuffed chintz sofas in a slatted barn. The intense green of summer shimmered through the cracks, giving a verdant glow to the scattered instrument cases, the stacks of sheet music, the clumps of whispering people. On stage, Anna's current lover, an influential cellist twenty-five years her senior, was playing a Bach solo sonata.

Across the barn, Heinrich Moulton, revered and beloved chamber musician and founder of the festival, paused and listened. The cellist played clearly, with a deep, rosined edge. His smooth bow, his slow vibrato, his firm fingers, rose like groans from a fenestrated sleep. Yes, thought Heinrich. If life is a dream, music is the sleep itself, the language before life, before dreams, the language of heartbeat, respiration, of blood as it squirts through the arteries and eddies and pools in our veins. He remembered, suddenly, his childhood nanny, the roses outside the gate that led to the house on Prinzregentenstrasse. He thought again of his own solitary survival, his new American life, with a wife and two sons, a position on the faculty of Juilliard, and a successful festival.

"Oh Heinrich," called Anna softly, "have you heard the terrible news?"

"What?" he said after Anna told him. "Lynette?" He felt an abrupt disorientation, as if the barn around him had disappeared, leaving him suspended in a cacophony of sound and motion. And then Heinrich Moulton, foreign for all his desperate and careful rebirth, still half-German half-Jew from Munich, then Paris, then Cuba, remembered, as one remembers first love, the precise way this unpleasant girl Lynette had played the Mozart Sinfonia Concertante in his small studio at Juilliard.

It was last winter, when it wasn't clear that the festival would get off the ground, and Heinrich was consumed with preparations and endorsements. Anna, who had signed up for second-semester chamber music, asked if she could bring her roommate for duets. Heinrich nodded absently.

"We'll do the Mozart Sinfonia Concertante," said Anna. "I'm thinking of switching to viola. Easier to get into a quartet, what do you think, Heinrich?" But Heinrich didn't answer. He was smiling, remembering the first time he had played this piece. His father, a violinist in the prewar Bavarian Orchestra, played viola at home, in deference to his small prodigy son. When nine-year-old Heinrich played the Sinfonia's opening salute, then burst into tears at hearing himself in the middle of that music, his father gently took away the half-size violin, put down his own viola, and sat Heinrich next to him on the couch.

"Yes," he said. "For you, like me, it will be this way. It is a gift without choice." So Heinrich looked forward to teaching the Mozart. He was completely unprepared for Lynette.

The girl pushed into his room on the third floor, swinging her hips in their short black miniskirt and her long legs around the piano, throwing her battered violin case across the arms of a wooden chair against the wall. "Hi," she said. Heinrich straightened the creases in his grey wool pants and didn't answer. But when Anna introduced him, he realized this Lynette was an Ivanovich student. She'd been mentioned in department meetings—a prize winner, but there was some problem. Laziness? Something Ivanovich, the chairman of the department, wanted to drop her for. Heinrich shrugged his shoulders. It was not his problem, not his student. And he certainly wasn't about to make it his business. He sat at the piano, opened the score, and smiled at the students. "So," he said, "we begin?" And he played the introduction, bouncing up and down, missing notes, and singing along with himself. "Now," he shouted, when it was time for the girls to enter, because he wasn't sure they could tell where he was. Then he heard.

It was the sweetest, most perfectly clear tone Heinrich had ever heard from a violin. Some rough spots, clearly unpractised and un-rehearsed, and then gorgeously light spiccato, subtle, mature, crystal-line notes, falling one after another, as if the idea of the music were so perfectly realized there was no violinist at all but just Mozart and himself, Heinrich, the listener. Heinrich sucked in his breath and closed his eyes, playing from memory, trying now, very hard, to play in a manner worthy of this sound. He frowned at the poor violist, Anna, who was merely very good. He cursed under his breath when this new girl, Lynette, stumbled over easy passages. And he felt pierced with pleasure, through his catalogue of selves—prominent New York musician, sophisticated man, German orphan—down to the unchanging part of himself that was his father's son, when she got it right.

After they stopped, Heinrich sat for a few minutes without talking. Then he made several reasoned suggestions, and, smiling distantly, scheduled another lesson. He did not say to Lynette: you are astounding, your playing cracks the concrete in my soul, you are one in a million, the real thing, I am in your debt. Instead, he felt angry, annoyed that she had stripped him in this way when he had so much of the dailiness of life on his mind. He closed his violin case, locked the studio, and took a long walk down Claremont Avenue, over to Broadway, past the back of Juilliard, the tenements, the Spanish grocery, up into Harlem, watching his feet and the sky, remembering certain passages, hearing the sound again, her sound, clutching it to himself in secret pleasure. He walked until his feet hurt, and the chill of the February day finally made him realize he wore only a sport coat and needed to return.

That night he said to his wife, "This festival is important backup. It's essential that I have a name, an income, a reputation separate from Ivanovich. Some day he might decide he doesn't care for me, after all. And for now, it means more for the boys' trust funds, just in case."

"Henry," said his wife, who called him that because he asked her to, "it's not Germany, it's not wartime."

"In Germany," said Heinrich, "before it was wartime, it was first not wartime."

The next time Heinrich met with Lynette and Anna, he was more prepared. He went over each line of the first movement, rigorously, showing the chords and the harmonic progressions on the piano, singing the shaping of the lines, making them work, and work. In the end, the music rose beyond his expectation, like a beaten silver moon casting nets across the Starnbergersee, seizing him in the textures of childhood. Heinrich was unable to fully restrain himself and said, "If the two of you wish to perform this, I can find a place for you to play."

Anna looked at Lynette, who put down her violin and took out a cigarette. Lynette said, "Ivanovich is trying to get rid of me. He says things like, I can't keep every student, and, you better work hard for your jury." She lit the cigarette and stared at Heinrich.

"Lynette," said Anna, "don't smoke here."

"Maybe," said Heinrich, "you are just imagining it." Neither girl spoke.

"She's lazy," said Anna, after a minute. "And she doesn't care that he sees her with boys."

"Are you not," said Heinrich to Lynette, "allowed boyfriends?"

Anna laughed. "With Ivanovich," she said, "it's bad enough if you're a girl. You're not allowed anything else."

"You waste everyone's time," said Heinrich, "if you do not practice."

Lynette looked at the floor, pressing her lips together. Heinrich saw that under the make-up she was young. Sixteen perhaps, or seventeen. He felt a sudden sorrow. "If you wish," he grunted, "I will tutor you for your jury."

"The girl," said one of Ivanovich's assistants, whom Heinrich had asked the next day, "is a little whore. No discipline, no foundation. You'll get tired of her, if she doesn't get pregnant first."

"Sometimes," said Heinrich, "it is the undisciplined ones that are the best."

"Ivanovich is thinking," said the assistant, "of stopping accepting girls at all. Too much trouble."

When Anna and Lynette got back to their studio apartment, Anna sat on the bed and looked at Lynette until Lynette stopped and said, "What?"

"What do you think?" said Anna. "Rent?"

"God, I'm sorry," said Lynette. "I'll have it next week."

"I try to get you jobs," said Anna, "and you don't show up. Or you don't dress right."

"I guess," said Lynette, beginning to cry, "I should just quit."

"Oh Christ," said Anna, who was two years older, "there's a job up in Yonkers next week. With Michael Rubin, who, by the way, thinks you're going to win the Leventritt over him. You can have it, but you better show up."

"Sure," said Lynette. "Thanks."

"What about the Leventritt?" said Anna.

Lynette shrugged her shoulders. "I get," she said, "too nervous to practice. I feel like a jerk." She began to bite her nails.

Anna watched her. "Some of us," she said vehemently, "work our butts off and never get a break." She stamped into the hall. "By the way, what happened to the cookies my mother sent?" Lynette leaned against the wall. She rubbed her eyes and reached for another cigarette.

Anna thought of the cookies, how her mother had tied them with a bow and covered the wrap with little hearts. "Never mind," she said suddenly. She'd never seen any of Lynette's family. Once a friend of Lynette's father came through town and looked Lynette up. Anna came in the apartment to find them on the floor, his dirty hands against Lynette's honey-colored skin, holding her as she struggled and wept. Anna had shouted at him and threatened to call the police, until, finally, he pulled up his jeans, ran his hand through his thinning hair, and left. "I'm sorry," Lynette said to Anna later. "I know you're not used to that kind of stuff."

When Lynette called to schedule a lesson three weeks later, Heinrich didn't remember at first who she was. He had been working frantically to get endorsements of the festival; Ivanovich was mentioning it to former students, big-league soloists, and the bookings were starting to come in. Heinrich was careful to present himself to Ivanovich as an organizer, a teacher of chamber musicians, not soloists. He thanked Ivanovich many times and stressed how important he and his students were to Heinrich's efforts.

"Who?" he said after his wife gave him the phone in the kitchen. Then he remembered. Damn. And he had given her his home number. "Yes," he said, as she began to hesitate, "I will meet you once." And, yelling at his sons to be quiet so he could hear, he set the date. That is enough, he told himself. It is up to her what she does with it.

When she arrived for the lesson, he looked at her laddered black stockings, her vinyl skirt, her heavy make-up, and said nothing. But they worked hard on the concerti she was due to play. Heinrich could see she had not practiced.

"What will you do," he said, "if you do not pass your jury?"

Lynette didn't answer for a while. "I don't know," she said finally, "it's just a blank."

"Don't be melodramatic," said Heinrich, "you have your whole life ahead of you."

On violin jury day, Heinrich entered the performance room at eight in the morning with a cup of coffee and a donut. Ivanovich was already there and looked up. "Hello," he said. "I hear good things about the festival you plan." Heinrich flushed with pleasure. "It is always useful," said Ivanovich, "to have a place for my students to perform, get ready for the competitions."

"I'm very grateful," said Heinrich, "for your help." Ivanovich waved his hand dismissively and greeted two of his assistants, who had just entered the room.

There were eighteen violin students to judge, each with twenty minutes to play bits of a solo selection, and two concerti with piano accompaniment. After each performance, the four jury members discussed the strengths and weaknesses and decided on a grade. Lynette was twelfth, at two in the afternoon. The faculty were growing tired and testy after hearing the same Bach, the same Vieuxtemps, the same Paganini, the same Beethoven, without even time for more than a bag lunch. When Lynette came in, Heinrich felt the beginning of a headache. She wore a black leather skirt and a tight, almost transparent blouse. He looked away.

Her voice shook as she announced the Bach, the Beethoven, the Vieuxtemps. But when she put the violin up, closed her eyes, and began to play, Heinrich felt his heart stop. The pianist, a graduate student hired to do the jury accompanying, suddenly began to move, as if waking for the first time all day. Lynette played just as he had taught her. Heinrich's eyes filled with tears. "Yes," he wanted to shout. "Yes, yes, yes." As Lynette left, the pianist hurried after her for a moment, touching her arm gently and protectively as they went through the door.

"I will fail her," said Ivanovich. He and the two assistants marked "F" on their ballots. Heinrich did not move. Ivanovich looked at him. "She is lazy and promiscuous," he said.

"I thought there was some merit to her performance," Heinrich said.

"It is important," said Ivanovich, "for me to control my students.

Some students do not reflect well on the teacher." He paused. "I did hear you coached her. I was sorry to hear it."

Heinrich looked at Ivanovich, then at the two assistants. Even an "A" from him would not give the girl a passing grade. He felt a drop of sweat roll down his side. "Of course," he said. "It was a mistake, an enthusiasm of the moment." He picked up his pen and marked "F" on his ballot, then put the pen down and looked away. He found himself staring directly at the pianist as she returned to her seat. He looked away quickly, but not quickly enough. He had seen her shock, her fierce witness.

———

At these remembrances, Heinrich felt himself pale and tremble. He stood for a moment without speaking.

"Is there something wrong?" said Anna, rising to his side.

"How terrible," said Heinrich. "She was so young."

"No younger than us," said Michael.

"Yes," said Heinrich, looking at Michael and Anna and feeling overwhelmed by youth, sadness, and the business of music, "no younger than you."

That evening after the concert, he went out with the performers to a small cafe in Brattleboro. The subject of the girl Lynette passed quickly, and, after that, in the course of many amusing anecdotes, Heinrich drank too much wine and had to be driven home, with one of the students following behind in Heinrich's car.

"I am sorry," Heinrich apologized to his wife the next morning as she prepared his breakfast. But his wife, who was pulling boxes from the pantry, did not hear.

———

Ten years after Lynette died in a tide of blood and bewilderment, she passed into the mythology of Juilliard. Anna Mikolich, now divorced and on the teaching faculty, spoke of her only when asked. "Her playing was extraordinary," she would say to the students and leave it at that. Anna could not formulate the rest, but it came to her as she sat, alone, in the living room of her Central Park West apartment, touching the silk upholstery on the couch or walking barefoot on the Persian rug. At these times she would feel herself changed, hammered, soldered and welded by the years and acts of competition. She would think about music, the children she feared she would not have, and she would think about Lynette.

Michael Rubin, on the other hand, eventually won the Leventritt and developed an erratic solo career. When the subject of Lynette arose, he shook his head. She killed herself, he said mournfully. Such a pity. Such a talent, straight from God. But as he lay in bed at night and remembered the passion of her music, he knew she had been the same kind as he. And a sudden coat of fear would shimmer over the dimmed elements of the room: bedposts, nightstand, dresser, like an ice storm in his mind.

Heinrich Moulton, an exuberant fifty-five, was at the peak of his powers. The festival had become an enormous success, so successful that Heinrich no longer had much time to perform or even teach, and required a battery of assistants. And that fall, despite the added staff, he found the festival overbooked.

"I'm not sure we'll be able to find a place for those last two students of yours," he said to Ivanovich casually, as they passed in the hall at Juilliard.

Ivanovich stopped. His hair had turned white, his face drooped with age. "Excuse me?" he said, frowning.

Heinrich smiled. "You know," he said pleasantly, "we never expected it, but with all the applications from Paris and Moscow, not to speak of Indiana, we just got overbooked." He shrugged his shoulders and began to move on.

"I'm sure," said Ivanovich, "you can find a way." The Vermont Festival was a desirable proving ground for Ivanovich's young soloists, a pleasant and prestigious summer venue for the established performers. In addition, many of his students now felt chamber-music training critical to their careers.

"Well," said Heinrich, still smiling, "it's not so easy. The deposits are already accepted." He tried again to move down the hall.

"Those boys are very talented," said Ivanovich, growing red. "You are making a mistake."

"Talent," said Heinrich, "isn't everything." He thought of the debts he owed the major teachers at each of several conservatories, the favors done for him by a number of famous soloists.

"Talent," shouted Ivanovich, "*is* everything. You are making a mistake." He turned from Heinrich, entered the violin department office, and slammed the door.

Heinrich stood looking at the green paint of the closed door, slightly surprised. He thought of his own recent interviews on television, the reviews and articles in the *New York Times*. Ivanovich, he concluded, was jealous. Heinrich strode down the hall. He would take those Ivanovich students whose careers would profit the Festival, and only those. Let Ivanovich worry about the rest.

When he repeated the conversation to his wife that evening, Heinrich slapped his thighs and chuckled. "Imagine," he said. "How things have changed."

His wife sighed. "Are you sure, Henry," she said, "that you are being fair to the students? They didn't ask to be caught in a fight between you and Ivanovich."

"Who said it was a fight?" said Heinrich.

"I always thought," said his wife, who had curled, since the boys were grown, into her novels and arthritis, "that there was something special about music. Something you should treat with more respect."

"Bullshit," said Heinrich. "Music is a business, like any other business."

"What about your father," said his wife, "and that girl, Lynette?"

"Do you think," shouted Heinrich, "we bought this house with sentimentality?"

"Never mind," said his wife, rolling her eyes and going back to her novel.

As it happened, that summer Anna Mikolich and Michael Rubin were once again to perform at the Vermont Music Festival. Heinrich arrived with his wife the second week of July. Where it had been, already, unbearably hot in New York, it was still cool in Vermont. The grass of the festival grounds was a particularly brilliant green; the peonies lining the barn and the walkways, a glossy hedge garnished with opulent pink and red blossoms.

"Isn't it beautiful," said Michael, standing with Heinrich and Anna before the barn.

"We have a marvelous season planned," said Heinrich, clapping his hands and rising on his toes. "Outstanding."

"Do you remember," said Anna, "the last time we were here together?"

"No," said Michael.

"It was," said Anna, "the summer Lynette died." Anna glanced around, then said, confidentially, "They should have kicked Ivanovich out for that."

"Why?" said Heinrich, clamping his lips together. "No one forced her to get pregnant. No one forced her to have an abortion."

"If Ivanovich had gotten her a sponsor," said Anna, "like he did for all the boys. Money to live on. She'd already won San Francisco, don't you remember?"

"I remember," said Michael, "that you were booked as replacement before the rest of us could even dial our agents."

"And you," said Anna, "finally did win the Leventritt, didn't you?"

"It's not the teacher's responsibility," broke in Heinrich, "to look after the private lives of students."

"She was," said Anna, "sixteen."

"When I was sixteen," said Michael, "I still thought that music was an art." He laughed.

"Did you know she was *failed* on her last jury?" said Anna. She watched a beetle crawl across the path and ground it viciously under her toe. "No one protected her," she said, "not even me." She began to cry.

Annoyed, Heinrich excused himself and walked away. He looked at the orderly lines and squares of peonies, at the carpetlike thick lawns and the precise demarcations where lawn turned to wild meadow. A breeze played over the meadow grass, stirring it into a gentle rippling as the adjacent lawn lay motionless. Look how far I have come, he told himself, an orphan. A family, this festival, students. Look what I have built, by myself, from nothing. But when Heinrich got home, he took out the scotch and began to drink.

In the evening, Anna and Michael came for dinner. Heinrich motioned to them without getting up. "Henry's feeling," his wife said, catching the glances that passed between them, "a little tired."

"When I was a boy," Heinrich told Anna and Michael, as they sat after dinner, "my father disappeared of his own will. He was Catholic but born a Jew. He sent my mother, who was blond as I am, to live with me in Paris. He made this sacrifice to save my mother's life." Heinrich poured himself another scotch.

"Let's move," said his wife, "to the living room for coffee and dessert." Anna and Michael shifted their feet and smiled politely.

Later in the evening Michael asked, "What happened to your mother after your father disappeared?"

"After that," said Heinrich, "my mother died."

That night, Heinrich fell asleep without difficulty, but later, as the moon rose through the lace curtains of the bedroom, he awoke shaking and wet with sweat. He got up and took out his violin. He rubbed it against his cheek. He stared at the curved outline, the glossy finish, the coiled scroll and thought about the girl, Lynette. I was new on the faculty, he told himself. I had my own family to consider. She was loud, promiscuous, and difficult. Heinrich put the violin away and went back to sleep.

The next day began still, hot, and humid, waiting for a storm. Heinrich arose early, took his coffee, and walked up to the barn to listen to the orchestra rehearse Tchaikovsky's Serenade for Strings. He felt the warmth of the air and the music caressing the meadow. The Tchaikovsky needed work, but there was time. The publicity was out, and the sales were doing well. How fortunate I am, he thought, to have all this, this music, this meadow, this festival.

When Heinrich entered the hall, he saw that the students had stopped and were preparing to play another piece. He frowned. Anna and Michael stood before the orchestra. Michael had a viola.

"Heinrich," called Anna. "We were just going to play the Mozart Sinfonia Concertante." She smiled at him and laughed. "For fun."

"And are you all so prepared for the concert that you can afford to spend your time fooling around?" said Heinrich. He turned on his heel and walked down to the second row. There was a momentary quiet in the hall. Anna stared at Heinrich, a faint crease across her forehead. Michael looked at the floor and swung his viola gently back and forth. Finally, as Anna turned to face the orchestra, the violins, of their own accord, began.

Heinrich heard the E-flat chords, then the rhythmic spiccato. He sighed loudly and buried his face in his hands. He sat there for a moment, feeling a swell of intense, almost unbearable irritation. Out on the meadows humidity ruptured and it started to rain. Heinrich found himself becoming short of breath. Over the rain, against his will, he felt the cellos invade his skin, the violins on his tongue. He heard the familiar and beautiful opening salute, the solo violin and viola arc above the orchestra. Playing in unison, Anna and Michael turned to each other intimately. Outside, the rain quieted, drops coalescing off the roof into membranous sheets. Listening to Michael, his ringing, rounded tone, Anna closed her eyes and smiled. The students in the orchestra rested their heads against their instruments and seemed, still playing, to pass into sleep. Heinrich began to tremble with anger.

"Here, Heinrich," said Anna, stopping the music by tapping her bow against the stand. She held her violin out toward him and said gently, "You play."

"Does no one here," shouted Heinrich, "consider that we have sold tickets to a concert for which you are not prepared?" Flushed with fury, Heinrich rose and left, without a coat or hat, directly into the rain.

He spent the afternoon wrapped in a blanket on the living room couch. He reviewed the festival's books: tuition, scholarships, payment to faculty and staff, the refreshment concession, ticket sales. He balanced accounts with satisfaction, smoothing each page and writing totals in a neat, precise hand. The sense of financial security calmed him. When he finished, he sat and stared at the wall.

That evening, Heinrich stood in the kitchen, watching his wife peel potatoes for dinner. "I invited Anna and Michael again," said his wife. "I think Anna wants to help you with the administration. I think she admires the way you have built a career."

"I did not set out," said Heinrich, "to become anyone's model." And he looked at his hands, the hands that had tended his mother in the typhus epidemic of the displaced person's camp, that had made his musical career in America, that had made him famous. He saw that they were old, the veins knotted and circuitous. "This morning," he said, "they played the Sinfonia Concertante."

"Here," said his wife, handing him a potato and peeler, "if you're going to stand there, do something useful."

Heinrich began to slice skin from the potato, watching the sheen of the blade against the dusty brown. He saw the long peel strip away, again and again, revealing the moist white underneath, as if his right arm, unbidden, were bowing a martelé exercise from childhood. He relaxed.

"Do you think," said his wife, "it's really going to rain again?"

"Maybe," said Heinrich. He watched the faint dent of the metal pressed for the next slice. "And maybe not," he added. And then he watched himself drive the sharpened blade of the peeler directly across the tip of his left middle finger, severing the fleshy pad.

The finger bled profusely, spraying and splattering a fine red mist across Heinrich and his wife. "I think," said his wife, holding it tightly with a kitchen towel, "we should go to the hospital in Brattleboro."

It took over an hour for the surgeon to suture Heinrich's finger. As the nurse taped gauze carefully across the wound, Heinrich looked up. The surgeon, who had attended the festival and knew who Heinrich Moulton was, avoided his eye. "Tell me," said Heinrich, when the nurse finished.

"We'll wait and see," said the surgeon.

"Will I be able to feel? I must feel the string to play," said Heinrich.

The surgeon paused and colored. Heinrich's wife rested her hand, lightly, on his shoulder. "No," said the surgeon. "The nerve is dead."

Heinrich felt a sudden stillness. He stared at the white cotton curtain that divided him from the rest.

"Do you have any other questions?" asked the surgeon, sitting on a stool.

"It doesn't matter," said Heinrich. And he got up to leave, because he had heard everything there was to hear. He had heard the music and the stillness. He had heard the tongue and thread of God.

Heinrich pushed open the curtain. "Please," he said to his wife, "would you drive me home?" Then, holding his ruined hand, he walked out into the cool night air.

The students sat murmuring in the back of the music barn.

"Michael," said Anna, who was leaning against a wood beam. "Have you heard the terrible news about Heinrich?"

"Oh my God," said Michael, when she told him. "Why? Why Heinrich?"

"Accidents happen," said Anna sadly.

"Someone," said Michael, "will need to run the festival. Someone who can play and attract students." He looked at his own trembling fingers. "Not me," he said.

"Yes," said Anna. "It would be good to have a name, a reputation separate from Heinrich. After all, I am a single woman and not getting any younger." She moved away from Michael. He was lazy, she suddenly realized, and undisciplined. She would be new at running a festival and had her own future to secure.

The Iowa Short Fiction Award and John Simmons Short Fiction Award Winners

1994
The Good Doctor,
Susan Onthank Mates
Judge: Joy Williams

1994
Igloo among Palms,
Rod Val Moore
Judge: Joy Williams

1993
Happiness, Ann Harleman
Judge: Francine Prose

1993
Macauley's Thumb, Lex Williford
Judge: Francine Prose

1993
Where Love Leaves Us,
Renée Manfredi
Judge: Francine Prose

1992
My Body to You, Elizabeth Searle
Judge: James Salter

1992
Imaginary Men, Enid Shomer
Judge: James Salter

1991
The Ant Generator,
Elizabeth Harris
Judge: Marilynne Robinson

1991
Traps, Sondra Spatt Olsen
Judge: Marilynne Robinson

1990
A Hole in the Language,
Marly Swick
Judge: Jayne Anne Phillips

1989
Lent: The Slow Fast,
Starkey Flythe, Jr.
Judge: Gail Godwin

1989
Line of Fall, Miles Wilson
Judge: Gail Godwin

1988
The Long White,
Sharon Dilworth
Judge: Robert Stone

1988
The Venus Tree,
Michael Pritchett
Judge: Robert Stone

1987
Fruit of the Month, Abby Frucht
Judge: Alison Lurie

1987
Star Game, Lucia Nevai
Judge: Alison Lurie

1986
Eminent Domain, Dan O'Brien
Judge: Iowa Writers' Workshop

1986
Resurrectionists, Russell Working
Judge: Tobias Wolff

1985
Dancing in the Movies,
Robert Boswell
Judge: Tim O'Brien

1984
Old Wives' Tales, Susan M. Dodd
Judge: Frederick Busch

1983
Heart Failure, Ivy Goodman
Judge: Alice Adams

1982
Shiny Objects, Dianne Benedict
Judge: Raymond Carver

1981
The Phototropic Woman,
Annabel Thomas
Judge: Doris Grumbach

1980
Impossible Appetites,
James Fetler
Judge: Francine du Plessix Gray

1979
Fly Away Home, Mary Hedin
Judge: John Gardner

1978
A Nest of Hooks, Lon Otto
Judge: Stanley Elkin

1977
The Women in the Mirror,
Pat Carr
Judge: Leonard Michaels

1976
The Black Velvet Girl,
C. E. Poverman
Judge: Donald Barthelme

1975
*Harry Belten and the
Mendelssohn Violin Concerto*,
Barry Targan
Judge: George P. Garrett

1974
*After the First Death There Is No
Other*, Natalie L. M. Petesch
Judge: William H. Gass

1973
The Itinerary of Beggars,
H. E. Francis
Judge: John Hawkes

1972
The Burning and Other Stories,
Jack Cady
Judge: Joyce Carol Oates

1971
*Old Morals, Small Continents,
Darker Times*,
Philip F. O'Connor
Judge: George P. Elliott

1970
The Beach Umbrella,
Cyrus Colter
Judges: Vance Bourjaily
and Kurt Vonnegut, Jr.